Song of Ascent

Song of Ascent

Stories by
Gabriella Goliger

RAINCOAST BOOKS

Vancouver

Raincoast Books acknowledges the ongoing support of the Canada
Council; the British Columbia Ministry of Small Business, Tourism
and Culture, through the BC Arts Council; and the Government of
Canada through the Book Publishing Industry Development Program
(BDIDP).

First published in 2000 by
Raincoast Books
9050 Shaughnessy Street
Vancouver, B.C.
V6P 6E5
(604) 323-7100

www.raincoast.com

Edited by Joy Gugeler
Cover design by Les Smith
Cover photo by Maria Coletsis

CANADIAN CATALOGUING IN PUBLICATION DATA
Goliger, Gabriella, 1949-
Song of ascent
ISBN 1-55192-374-2
I. Title.
PS8563.O82848S66 2000 C813'.6 C00-910712-6
PR9199.3.G5995S66 2000

Printed and bound in Canada

°00 01 02 03 04 05 1 2 3 4 5

For my loving family and friends
and especially for my parents

Song of Ascent

Breaking the Sabbath

Throughout her long life Hannah Birnbaum, née Teilheimer, has remembered in detail a hiking trip she took by herself through the Giant Mountains near her home-town of Breslau, shortly before she left Germany for good.

It was September 1933 and she was 18. Hitler had come to power at the beginning of the year. There'd been the boycott of Jewish businesses, the burning of the books, quotas on Jews in the civil service and in universities. Everyone in her youth group was talking emigration.

But it was mainly due to her sister Edith that the walk in the mountains etched itself into Hannah's memory. Just as Hannah had been about to reach the summit of Schneekoppe, the highest peak on the German side of the border with Czechoslovakia, she had a premonition. It happened in an instant, the sense of dread, unaccountable, yet as sharp as the taste of blood on the tongue. She was not a believer in such things — voices, visions — nevertheless, after some hesitation, she had turned in her tracks and commenced the long trudge downward through the pine-skirted slopes, her legs sore and heavy, all the joy of exploration drained from her limbs.

For once, Hannah had no trouble deflecting her father's questions about where she was going. She lifted her eyes to the photograph of her mother, the lady in white on the mantelpiece, and said, "I'd like to spend *Shabbat* with Gerda." An inspired half-truth. Her cousin, Gerda Rott, lived across town on the other side of the river and Gerda's family kept the Sabbath with as much rigour as Hannah's father did. But it was another Gerda — Gerda Levittson, her comrade in the Zionist youth group — whom Hannah had in mind.

Edith, who was pushing cabbage rolls around on her plate, caught on immediately. Her eyes flicked between Hannah and their father, her mouth twisted in a smirk. Eliezer continued to chew chopped egg and challah and to wipe crumbs with a nervous hand from his stiff, black mous- tache.

"I'll stay over Sunday. I'll be home...."

"Yes, yes. Fine," Eliezer waved his napkin at her.

It clearly didn't occur to him to put the Levittsons and *Shabbat* together since, as far as Eliezer was concerned, they were merely liberal Jews, part of the godless majority that had forsaken the Covenant. Mr. Levittson conducted business on the day of rest, while his son, Gerda's older brother Ludwig, was known as a reckless prankster and a lady's man. For Hannah, Gerda's home was a refuge, a place where one could listen to the radio on Saturday and where one could still eat meat, despite the ban on kosher slaughtering. The Levittsons had always bought from the gentile butcher any- way. A Sabbath with the Levittsons was freedom, but this Saturday she'd be freer still. She and Gerda had plans.

Dinner continued in silence. There was rarely talk at the Friday-night table unless Eliezer initiated it himself. He would direct his voice over his daughters' heads and at the tender-eyed photo on the mantelpiece. Sometimes he told jolly stories about the farmers who still came to his warehouse to buy grain sacks and cider barrels. Mostly he ranted. Not about the socialists any more, since they'd been cleared off the streets with a speed that took even Eliezer aback. No, nowadays he heaped his scorn mainly upon Hitler's shameless louts and upon the secular Zionists. He had nothing against a return to Zion, but the wrong kind of Jews were returning. "Socialists with Stars of David on their chests...defilers of the Sabbath."

That evening, though, Eliezer was content to fume in silence, his lips twitching, his eyes smouldering with grievances. Hannah relaxed and devoted herself to her meal, but became alarmed when she glanced at Edith. Her sister was frowning and muttering expressions of disdain into her plate, performing a perfect parody of their father.

"*Lumpenpack*...scoundrels," she scolded the untouched bundles of cabbage and rice.

Hannah kicked her under the table. "Stop it," she mouthed. Edith's lips twisted into a half smile, part apology, part defiance.

"Edith, for heaven's sake, eat," Hannah said out loud. "You're getting worse and worse. How can you expect to fill out if you don't eat?"

She'd being saying these words day after day for years. Hannah knew, of course, that Edith didn't expect to fill out. Her sister was convinced she was destined to be a runt and held to this view with what seemed almost perverse satisfaction. At 14 she still had the same difficulty with food that she'd had as a baby, indifferent at best, squeamish about anything that was the least bit unfamiliar. Often, she regarded her plate with anger and loathing. She didn't merely flatten and rearrange her mound of turnips, she stabbed at it and plunked the burdensome forkfuls onto Hannah's plate. She whispered her father's repertoire of insults, mocking him, mocking herself, walking the thin edge of catastrophe.

She'd become odd. She practised what she called her "disappearing act," standing close to walls, sitting so still in a corner of a room that people walked in and out without noticing her. Meanwhile, she watched everyone else with eyes ancient as a cat's. She roamed the city by herself in her long, baggy coat, waiflike and pathetic. Scattered on the dresser of the bedroom they shared, Hannah found tram ticket stubs for routes in unfamiliar suburbs.

"What on earth were you doing there?" Hannah asked, but Edith merely shrugged.

"It's not safe these days to wander about like that. Don't you know what's going on out there on the streets?"

And then came Edith's inevitable answer, "Who'd want to bother with little old me?"

Hannah worried, but she lost patience, too. And sometimes Edith's disappearing act was so effective Hannah forgot all about her.

When Edith was a baby, Hannah hovered about the crib, sang her favourite songs to the pale, grublike infant that stared and sucked its fist. Edith would cry, not loudly but steadily, until Tilly, the maid, seized her from the cradle and pushed a fat red forefinger into the baby's mouth. Hannah, five years old, took baby Edith onto her lap along with the knitted bedjacket that their mother used to wear. It was still laid out on the bed in her old room, a fine, cream-coloured wool from before the war, smelling faintly of *eau de cologne* and warm to the touch. Hannah wrapped the sleeves around Edith's neck.

"Mother loves you even if you're a small and miserable package," Hannah cooed. She piped, *"Hänschen klein...ging allein*...little Hansie, went out alone, into the wide, wide world."

Their mother was dead, no longer locked into that narrow, wasted body in the bedroom. Her spirit had been freed to spread through the house, infuse itself into the tile stove, cuckoo clock, feather comforters, everything that didn't have their father's stamp on it. During her mother's illness, Hannah was rarely allowed into the sick room, but she knew that the woman on the bed was shrinking like storybook Kaspar who wouldn't eat his dinner. In her dreams Hannah was terrified of crushing her cricket-size mother under her own ungainly duck feet. Puny Edith had something of their diminished mother about her. In Edith's small, serious face and limp neck, their mother's suffering was reborn.

At one time, Edith had craved her father's attention. When very young, she would charge into the library and tumble at his feet while he stood at morning prayers. Wrapped in his prayer shawl and phylacteries, his gaze remained fixed on the prayer book held stiffly before him and his voice droned on, the words like stones churning round and round in his mouth. Hannah hurried into the room to pull Edith away, but still caught her father's irate glare, the jerk of his chin indicating the door.

Dinner was over. It had proceeded through its various courses, mercifully, without outburst. The tedious "Grace after Meals" had also come to an end. Their father was in his study and Hannah was able to pack her knapsack. Two glorious days of hiking, singing, dancing lay before her. There'd also be discussions about politics and religion everyone could take part in, even an ignoramus like herself. How had she lived before the Blau-Weiss, the Zionist youth group?

It had been mere existence, not a life, a tearful daily struggle with her secretarial job at the Warburg Bank. She had no talent for the work and had the job only because of the intercession of an uncle. She had tried to learn to type. Her blunt fingers thumped down on the keyboard so that a cluster of keys flew up and locked together in a frozen embrace. Mistakes in every sentence, gouges where the keys had smacked too hard and torn the paper. She saw sly smirks on the other girls' faces while their cool, white hands tripped over the keys. Her inner voice scolded, "Clumsy cow. Worthless. Useless." If only the supervisor would notice her agony and give her another task or show her the door. It was a busy time: a run on accounts; a flurry of deposits; people wavering, waiting to see what the regime would do next.

And then Gerda brought her to the Reform synagogue to hear a young rabbi deliver a talk about the Jewish home-land. Forbidden territory, this building with the wide steps, the Romanesque arches, the organ pipes glimmering under stained-glass windows. Her father called it "the temple of sin." She didn't care for services, even the Reform version, but she was happy for an excuse to tread upon unholy ground. Throughout the talk, Gerda kept Hannah's arm tucked under her own and squeezed it when the rabbi made salient points. She needn't have. The moment he began to speak, a veil lifted and suddenly Hannah saw the world in clear, sharp relief. Of course, of course. The Zionists had everything: ideals of equality and brotherhood, a perfect, unborn country and an answer to the circular arguments about whether one was a German of Jewish faith or a Jew of German citizenship or a total alien. A Jewish homeland across the wide, blue Mediterranean, far from the tired hatreds of Europe, far from her father's house.

After the talk, the young people — girls and boys she knew from school days — formed a circle and danced the *hora* to music from a scratchy record on the gramophone. Although Hannah couldn't quite manage the steps, her legs flew. She leapt into the whirl of motion, the stamp of feet, the intoxicating charge into the centre of the ring.

As Hannah rummaged in her drawer for matching stockings, she became aware of a mournful sound coming from inside the great armoire — a stifled warbling that raised the hairs on the back of her neck. She yanked open the door. The whole closet rattled.

"Edith, you gave me a fright. Why didn't you say something? And why can't you play a more cheerful tune? It sounds like a graveyard."

Edith was crouched on the floor of the armoire, her recorder on her knees.

"I'm trying to be quiet. And it was a cheerful song. It was 'The Miller's Wandering Song,' to get you into the mood for your trip."

Hannah hated it when Edith played her music in the closet. For some reason it set her on edge. And yet she knew she wasn't being fair. Where else could Edith play on the Sabbath? Their father's study was only two rooms away.

"Come out and talk to me instead of hiding in your cave. Anyway, I have to get in there and find my blue skirt."

Edith raised an arm and plucked the blue skirt off its hanger as if it were an apple. She unfolded her limbs and emerged, blinking in the room's electric light. Then she sat on her bed, arms around her knees, watching, while Hannah searched for missing underpants, a spare handkerchief, her good wool vest. Hannah found herself humming under her breath as she packed. "Oh, the miller loves to wander, loves to wander." The stirring old tune lodged itself in her head.

"Two whole days in the mountains," she exulted, but then stopped with the stab of guilt. Edith had to go to school. Edith would be alone with their father.

"You know, you really should join the Blau-Weissers. There's a group of younger ones your age. If only you'd give it a try."

Edith jumped up and began to cavort, Hassidic style, around the room, arms in the air, eyes half closed. She sang a satirical song in Yiddish that Hannah remembered from her own school days.

"*Oi wie faen wird es saen...*
Oh how fine it will be when the Messiah comes
We will build a land of paper
We will all march together
Oi, yoi, yoi, yoi."

Edith bleated out "*oi yoi*" in a high, nasal voice, so convincing that Hannah couldn't help but laugh.

"Stop it," she said, between gasps. "You've got it all wrong. That's the old, anti-Zionist propaganda. For one thing they're not all Polish Jews any more. There are lots of German Jews, too. More of us every day."

But Edith could not be reasoned with. "They don't want a scrawny mouse like me. I'm not built to be a pioneer," she said.

"No, no. We're both going to Palestine together," said Hannah, but it was hard to sound convincing in the face of Edith's stick arms and legs and her pale, pinched face.

A tap at the door. It was Tilly come to switch off the light, one of the innumerable forms of labour forbidden on the Sabbath. The two sisters undressed in the dark, snuggled under their featherbeds, and immediately Hannah drifted into a dream about the journey to come. She saw herself arm in arm with Gerda, marching down a country road under a broad and brilliant sky.

Hannah jumped out of bed while the room was still submerged in darkness. She planned to slip out before dawn, before her father was up. Edith would make up a story about why she'd left early. Or perhaps he wouldn't ask, too intent on rushing out the door and scurrying to the backroom prayer house where he met with his cohorts for the Sabbath-morning service. She dressed as quietly as she could, but Edith stirred, muttered something and stuck out a leg from under the blankets.

"Shh, Edie, go back to sleep."

"I have to get to school."

"It's not six o'clock yet."

"I have to sneak out with my books. I forgot to leave them yesterday."

"Oh, for heaven's sake, Edith."

Every Saturday, the dilemma of the schoolbooks. It was the law of the Sabbath that Edith carry nothing, not even a handkerchief, when she went out of the house. It was the law of the land that she go to school on Saturdays. Both laws must be obeyed. Eliezer could see no reason to change, even in these days of uncertainty and trouble when it was best not to draw attention to oneself.

"In every generation there are those who rise up against us," Eliezer quoted from the Haggadah with sour triumph.

And yet, he declared, generations of Teilheimers and Rotts and Goldsteins had managed. Orthodox children had gone to state schools to receive a decent, thorough, German education while keeping the laws of the Covenant. They brought their own food on school outings, refrained from writing and carrying on Saturdays and, of course, were often tormented for it. But some teachers had been most under-standing. Eliezer spoke fondly of his own master, Herr Kraus, a retired cavalry officer, who appreciated the extra discipline the Jews demonstrated, their unquestioning obedience to orders from on high. For years, Edith had a *Shabbas goy*, a Christian schoolmate who had carried her books on the Sabbath, since Eliezer would not allow any of the non-observing Jewish children to do it. But this year the girl had announced, chin in the air, that a pure-blooded German must not serve as mule for the Jew.

"Please, Papa. Relax the rules," Hannah had urged.

Eliezer had stared at her as if she'd lost her senses. He had his own solution, quite simple, really. The janitor would allow Edith to store her satchel in a cupboard in the school basement overnight on Fridays and pick it up in the morning. No one else had to know about the arrangement. The only problem was that Edith kept forgetting. She brought home her bag on Fridays and on Saturday morning had to endure a scene. Hannah doubted that Edith would creep quietly out of the house with her now. She would probably rouse Eliezer and his wrath would pour down upon them both

"Give me the bag, Edith. I'll pass by the school on my way to the train."

"But it's out of your way. You don't have to do that."

"Yes, yes. Get back into bed."

Edith mumbled her thanks and pulled the covers up around her ears. She hated the cold, especially the chill of early morning. Bookbag on one shoulder, knapsack on the other, Hannah slipped out of the dark apartment, down the stone stairway and into the street, where a fog greeted her. It smelled of river slime and coal dust.

The central train station rose massive and still in the early-morning light, the new flag with its swastika motionless over the portal. But stepping inside, Hannah was embraced by the familiar boom and bustle that always drove her heart a little faster. Her group was gathered on Platform 7 where the train for Waldenburg already waited, snorting steam. Each of her comrades carried a knapsack or bundle, each was dressed for the mountains in a warm jacket and sturdy shoes. Some held walking sticks, which they pumped against the platform floor.

There was Hugo, his face deep brown and scratched from baling hay. He'd already begun his farm training in preparation for a new life in Palestine. He planned to be off before the new year, to "redeem the land," as they said in the movement. He glanced at Hannah — a quick, warm look – and Liesel nudged Gerda. Hannah tried, but could not smile back in the open, friendly, no-nonsense way that would have been the right response. Neck stiff, suddenly aware of the largeness of her hands, she moved to the edge of the group. A tiny dart of pleasure twitched inside her. She calmed herself by surveying the platform scene.

A young porter stood nearby, one hand clasped around the handle of his upended trundle cart, the other hand holding a cigarette he seemed to have forgotten. A thin stream of smoke drifted up from between his fingers. He stared, eager and curious, at the cluster of Blau-Weissers before him. No one else seemed to notice him or the swastika that winked from his lapel — no armband or brown shirt, just the small square of red-and-black felt distributed at rallies. He continued to gaze at the centre of the group, trying to catch someone's eye. He was hoping for a friendly smile or wave, Hannah was sure of that. How often *she* had stared with pained longing before she'd found her place in the movement.

Would it dawn on him who they were? Would his soft, foolish longing harden into something else? She almost wished her friends would reveal themselves with a telling gesture or outlandish word. But of course they did not. If they spoke of movement affairs or used a Yiddish phrase it was *sotto voce*, speaking below the hiss of engines. The porter continued to stare and smile at fine German youth on an outing. For a moment, they all seemed frozen in their roles, like actors posing for a playbill; no one had any substance. And then, the train whistle blasted, the press of bodies boarded the train, the city slipped behind them and the gently rising countryside approached.

They slept at a farm outside the ancient resort town of Waldenburg. The youth hostels in the mountains might now be restricted, so it seemed safer to use the farmer's property (he was glad of the payment) as a base. Above the farm, hidden from view by the thick forest, the great mountain range stretched for 500 miles along the German-Czech border, spilling into both countries. Hannah had been on some of the lesser slopes during school day-trips, but never before had slept in mountain air, never been so long in the presence of the Giants.

They hiked along the trails single file, or three abreast when the path widened, their voices threaded together in song.

"*Anu holchim ba regel*...We go by foot, *hoppa, hoppa, hoppa, hey*," they shouted in Hebrew. Quickly exhausting their Hebrew repertoire, they launched into old German wandering songs. "Off To The Mountains In The Morning Dew," "Frankfurt I Must Leave You," "He Who Wanders with Purest Heart." In the evening they returned to the farm to cook potatoes and sausages in a campfire in the open field. At night, the girls retired to the barn, while the boys stayed outside beside the hayricks. There were more hopeful looks from Hugo, but Hannah stayed close to Gerda and the girls, content with the vague and pleasant glow created by the distance between them.

There were other times, though, when Hannah's skin prickled with frustration during the long-winded discussions and debates about strategy. How to comport oneself in the new Germany? How to explain that the Jews were a *Volk*, a people, just like the Germans, and loyal to their culture and state? And how to answer the criticism within their own community that they were merely playing into Hitler's hands by encouraging emigration to a new "ghetto" in the desert? The talk went on and on. It flared up, died down, began anew, arguments piling on top of one another. It broke the spell of the mountains and left Hannah weary and restless.

She lay in the hayloft that last night, listening to the snuffle of horses below. The thought of the journey home the next day gnawed at her. Their time was over before it had properly begun. Then it occurred to her that if she wasn't ready to leave, she didn't have to. The bank could do without her one more day. Before dawn she left a note in Gerda's shoe. "I've gone for one last ramble," she wrote. "I'll catch the three o'clock train back to town. Don't worry. I know my way."

She found the stairway leading from the road up the side of the mountain, into the cold, dark embrace of the forest. Goethe had walked here, tapping these very steps with his cane, had he not? Eichendorf had floated on the smell of fir, beech, birch and pine into one of his fairy stories. The hiking trail she wanted was marked with a stone pillar, the letters "S.K." for Schneekoppe — the highest peak of the range — engraved there, but she had to feel for their indented outline, like a blind woman, because of the pillar's fur of moss.

At first, she wondered whether she'd meet fellow wanderers and whether they'd greet her with the good cheer of old or glare with the suspicion one encountered everywhere now. But these thoughts soon dissolved in the pure mountain air. Trees blurred and billowed, their skirts danced in the breeze, branches touched. Each leaf took its turn on the wind. She walked and the old song sang in her head, the rhythm of the forest entered her feet.

"To wander, to wander, with spirit so free,
To follow the clouds, towards mountains and sea...."

She hummed, then sang out loud. Her limbs thrummed, her being expanded, she lost time and self, became one with the stirring of the pines.

After a while (she could not have said how long) she emerged from thick forest into low-growth alpine terrain. Below were lesser slopes, long deep valleys, meadows dotted with sheep, here and there a wisp of smoke, a strip of road. Continuing upward, she found herself enveloped in mist. The breath of the Giants swirled around her. Boulders lost their edges. Her hand disappeared when she stretched out her arm. Her feet found the trail, though her eyes could barely see it.

At a bend in the path she stopped. A crow cawed and then was silent. No wind, no sound except for the thumping in her ears. The mist luminous, opaque and strange. Was someone there, waiting, someone malicious? She held her breath. She strained to hear. Nothing. Nothing.

"Edith," she heard herself say out loud. "Edith."

Edith was in danger. She tried to dismiss the thought. She tried to conjure up her sister, drifting home from school through the park along the river, clutching her bookbag by its cracked leather strap. With each step she took, a sense of foreboding pressed harder against her heart. She turned back and hurried down the mountain.

Edith was already home from the hospital when Hannah arrived in town. Her arm was in a sling and half her face (the side on which her hair was parted) was greenish blue and swollen.

"I look like one of those decadent modern paintings," she said in a dull, far-off voice while passing the hall mirror. But she said little else and Eliezer, too, was tight-lipped, grim and distant.

Hannah learned about what had happened from Tilly in the kitchen. Edith had fallen out of the doorway of the Number 12 tram as it came hurtling around the road into Berliner Street. Miraculously, she'd sustained only minor injuries. The doctor said she would soon be as good as new.

"Herr Teilheimer could not understand what she was doing on a tram in the middle of the Sabbath," said Tilly, eyes wide with the horror of it. "He was called away from his afternoon Torah study."

"A terrible accident," Tilly hastened to add when Hannah stared at her.

At first Hannah thought it was the Hitler Youth. You didn't just fall out of a tram. Someone should at least tell the Centralverein, the Jewish community council, Hannah thought. These cases should be documented. But Eliezer glared at her when she made the suggestion and shook his head in disgust.

"And what about you," he growled. "I suppose you want me to believe you were kidnapped by the Sturmabteilung. Transported to the mountains!" He turned away, unable to bear the sight of her, and marched toward the coat stand. "Give my regards to cousin Gerda," he shouted as he slammed the front door.

After he left, the apartment became still and oppressive. How heavy and useless this old furniture — massive dining room table, brocade couch — appeared to Hannah after her walk among the pines. The living room was filled with a sad, grey light and from the grandfather clock in the hallway came a hollow *tick-tock* and the groan of metal. Although the living room seemed empty, Hannah knew Edith was there. The tired air, the listless drapes, spoke of her presence. Hannah waited a moment, then walked over to the windowsill.

"Edith," she said.

"Yes," came a toneless voice from behind the drapes. Hannah pulled aside the folds of fabric and there sat Edith in the wide bay window, resting her bandaged arm on her drawn-up knees. The undamaged side of her face was turned to the light and was as smooth and blank as carved stone. Hannah lowered herself beside her and began to pass her fingertips, as lightly as she could, over her sister's hair. Her big hand trembled as she touched, afraid of its weight, sensing the bruises hidden beneath the hairline. She took a deep breath.

"Did you jump or were you pushed?"

"Jumped."

"Oh, Edie. Why? Why?"

But Edith only shrugged and made a self-mocking grimace.

"Edith, Edele," Hannah crooned. "Promise me you'll never do this again. Promise me you'll come to the Blau-Weiss. And next year, after I've saved up the money, we'll go to Palestine together, you and me. We'll take the ship from Trieste across the Mediterranean Sea and every day it will be warmer and warmer. And then we will be with the

Haverim, the comrades. And you'll get suntanned and strong. Maybe even fat."

Edith smiled as she leaned her head against Hannah's shoulder. "You old donkey," she said.

On the street below, automobiles snorted and trams rattled by. Someone's hammer rang against a nail. The newsboy bawled out the headlines in a voice that was hoarse, but full of newfound zeal.

Song of Ascent

*I*n Jerusalem we lived on a roof.

"A view to die for," my mother said.

"An inferno. *Gehenna*," my father said. "Dangerous, too."

He was thinking not just of the months in 1948 when the shells rained down and the streets shook with explosions, but afterward, when snipers still took potshots from the Old City walls. It was the only place my parents could find. Many buildings had been reduced to bombed-out craters and the city lay divided by a jagged line of wall and barbed wire.

Although winters were cold and wet in Jerusalem and bitter winds raged around our little house, my parents remember the baking sun best, the cloudless days that lasted from May to October. In their stories and arguments it was always summer.

It was not exactly a *house* we lived in, but an addition of sorts, an afterthought, a simple whitewashed block of concrete and plaster. It consisted of two rooms and a galley kitchen perched on a broad, flat roof of a five-storey apartment building. It had been built, as had many others like it, for the stream of immigrants and refugees pouring into the country in the 1930s. Self-contained, the structure stood surrounded by water tanks, rusting bed frames, empty olive cans, cracked washtubs and odds and ends dumped there temporarily by other tenants. A few feet away from the entrance to our flat was our connection with the outside world, a door that led to the long, steep stairwell in the main building. No one standing below on Eden Street could have guessed our existence.

Seated on her stool in front of the door, a bowl of potatoes for peeling in her lap, my mother could see clear across the city, to other shacks on other roofs, to the domes, crosses, minarets, towers and the thick Crusader-era walls of the Old City where the Jordanian sentries stood. She could even see the Arab women's clotheslines strung along their rooftops, their sheets and *keffiyehs* stiffening in the sun.

Her view. Her roof. Fiercely hot to a bare-soled foot, seared by the relentless blaze from nine in the morning until five in the afternoon. Her plaza to walk about in, to wash clothes in before she hoisted me in her arms and headed off to clean houses in Rehavia.

"The sunsets over Jerusalem," she later recalled, a quaver in her voice. "The flowers." Spring anemones like tiny flames in the scrub fields between neighbourhoods.

"What about the flies? Hey?" my father would say. He would describe a pan of hummus he'd seen in the market, blackened with a solid layer of flies that lifted only when the bearded vendor dipped his cup into the paste, resettling to their feast an instant later.

Jerusalem of gold, Jerusalem of dust. Over the years, I reconciled the two sets of stories, became adept at entwining their complementary strands. Even today when I awake, terrified by an old dream in which I dangle by a thread over a gaping void, I listen in my mind for my parents' voices, speaking one on top of the other. I weave and weave their warring words into a net that holds us together and safe.

Every day at noon my father used to lug himself home from his job at the import company for lunch and a siesta. He trudged through crowded, clamorous streets, along fiery pavements, across roads gummy with half-melted asphalt, through air heavy with the stink of cheap petrol, rotting vegetables and beggars' spit. He arrived limp and drained at our building's stairwell, which was sweetly cool and dark on the first floor, warmer and brighter as he rose. Finally, he thrust his head into the white-hot glare, shielding his eyes against tormenting spears of light that glinted off metal flashings and wash buckets.

My older brother, Avi, would be home from kindergarten, directing his army of bottlecaps under the tin awning and I would be at play with my pan of water and my spoon. Father swooped each of us up, in turn, swung us around. He held me, then Avi, like a parcel high above his head, presenting us to the sky. But our moment of delight was short-lived. After a quick lunch, during which he chewed without appetite on his bread and omelette, he staggered into the shuttered bedroom and rolled onto the bed. There was no point in my mother chattering about her employer, Frau Doktor Mercaz, a woman who had an eagle eye for dust on the legs of the dining room table. He would shake his head, as if trying to shake free of something thickening around him, close his eyes and drift down, down into the well of suffocating sleep.

My mother, standing by the bedroom door, would see his fingertips twitch and his chin jerk, a gesture that seemed, though she knew he was asleep, to deliberately dismiss her. She would stir about the room, restless, open a dresser drawer and close it with a thud. She would pick me up and wander to the front door and back while my head drooped against her shoulder. At last, she settled me in my crib and sat down on the low wall that ran around the perimeter of the roof to look out over the city in the afternoon haze, the one time of the day the streets fell silent. She would fill her nostrils with the hot, dry air that went down like a gulp of brandy. The city — both sides — spread out before her, sun-scorched, salt-white. Her pulse throbbed with the dangerous heat. Another minute and she would have to seek shelter in her chair under the awning.

Let him sleep, she told herself. Let him turn his face to the wall. Let Frau Doktor mutter into her herring tidbits about the clumsy, inefficient help. She stared more intently at the city, lost herself in the tiers of houses that spilled down valleys, the weathered stones and hills, dazzling, incandescent pillars of salt under her gaze. In the distance, the mountains of Moab and Gilead danced against the sky.

My father had never been able to get used to the Middle Eastern heat. His blood was European, nurtured for generations by the fresh mountain chill of Bohemia. Nothing could be more foreign to him than the stupefying temperatures of his ancestral homeland. Low blood pressure, the doctor had said with a shrug. From the day he stepped off the boat, no, even before they reached shore, he'd felt a heaviness in his limbs and his eyelids, a clutching at his heart. For 17 years he fought the downward pull of drowsiness and when he did sleep, he awoke unrefreshed, head swimming. His ideals about the pioneering life dried up under the blistering sun. He'd planted orange trees, hacking at the stony ground with a short-handled hoe, shovelful by shovelful, stone by stone. His youth flaked off and fell into the parched earth, which he loosened, raked and watered with the feeble, rubber-tainted stream from the irrigation hose. The work at the import company was easier. There were shutters and ceiling fans. Still, sometimes it was all he could do to keep his head from lolling forward onto his typewriter. One day he looked up from the clatter of keys and out the window at the feet that tramped along the sidewalk. All seemed eager and energetic, while he sat like a frog too boiled to leap. A few more years and it would be too late.

Canada. The word was like a spring released. He met a Mr. Samson from Montreal whose smooth, pink cheeks advertised civilized climates, a startling contrast to the wrinkled, sun-ravaged faces of Jerusalem. Samson promised a job in his travel agency. He also promised that, within a year, they would have their own house and garden.

"That's how it is in Canada," he said, spreading his plump palms faceup.

My father didn't believe he would own a house and garden so quickly, but even if half of it were true, even a quarter, he told my mother, they would be better off. She crossed brown arms against her chest, her lips settled into a pout.

"Ha. You think everything will be golden. And if it doesn't work out? What will we do? Be stuck there, with nothing and no one."

"Other people succeed. Why shouldn't I?"

"Other people fail, too."

He saw her set against him. Her face, once so soft and carefree, now a knot of reproach. She was counting her disappointments over the years, hoarding them to shower upon his head. Despite this, one day he simply put it to her that he was leaving. She could come with him, or stay behind. The choice was hers.

We arrived in Montreal on a sweltering day in August and, after finding a place to stay near the railway station — a dark room with a smoke-streaked ceiling and one large, sagging bed for the four of us — sat in Dominion Square amid a swarm of pigeons. My mother scratched at a vicious heat rash that bubbled up on her arms and legs, an affliction she'd never had before. My brother counted buses, then streetcars, wide-eyed at the spray of sparks from the wires overhead. I gurgled and toddled after the pigeons. My father, head in his hands, willed away the panic in his chest. Senseless emotion.

A piece of newspaper in the wastebasket caught my mother's eye and she fished it out. She laboured over the headline. Ha, ha. Fate was having its joke, so she would laugh, would make him laugh. Why not? Ha, ha, ha. She would make him admit that she was not so ignorant of the world after all. My father glanced at the headline she thrust into his face. "Record heat wave hits: over 95 degrees in the shade." His gaze drifted past her to fix on the green-bronze statue — neither of them knew who it was — in the middle of the square. He said nothing for a few moments. Then, in a flat voice, "You think that would make the papers in Israel? Here it's an *event*."

After the rooming house, we bunked with the Fischbeins on Durocher, a street that people called the Borscht Alley. Two families in a two-bedroom apartment. Yankle Fischbein's shitty diapers in a pail on the kitchen floor. The windows steamed up from boiling cabbage. My mother and father hardly saw each other during those months. He worked from seven in the morning to after six in the evening for Samson the Swindler, while she worked in the apartment with the Fischbeins, all of them hunched over, holding metal punches, pressing rhinestones into bracelets for five cents a dozen. Under-the-table money.

At the end of the winter, my father finally found us an apartment of our own in a no-man's-land of newly developed lots between two older neighbourhoods, one classy, the other poor. He said it was a decent enough apartment on a decent enough street. There was a park nearby and a school. It was the first rung in a long ladder that might one day lead to a cottage on a lake in the Laurentians, Augusts spent with feet up on a deck chair in the shade of sweet-scented pines. Why not?

My father showed my mother around the new apartment: a master bedroom with a closet, small but separate rooms for Avi and me, an eat-in kitchen. The janitor, a man with a face as grey as his shirt, lounged against the wall outside the apartment door and smoked.

"Look at the size of the refrigerator," my father said. He ran a finger over the thick coat of frost under the freezer and tested the coolness of the clean, white walls.

"On the top floor, like you wanted, with a balcony."

A balcony indeed, my mother thought. It faced a laneway, a gravel parking lot and the backs of other squat, three-storey buildings, all shoulder to shoulder. The back door, as my father demonstrated, opened to a fire escape that led to a narrow, enclosed courtyard.

"Here's where we put out the trash," he said with a wave of his hand through the half-open door. He was about to close it again when my mother pushed past and stepped out onto the landing. A black metal stairway zigzagged downward past other back doors and bathroom windows. She sniffed the courtyard smells — damp cement, coal dust and garbage. Looking up, the sides of the building formed a chute with a rectangle of sky at the top. A breeze eddied dead leaves in the eaves troughs.

My father worked. While Samson drummed up business over lunch and cigars at the delicatessen, my father sat with the phone pressed against his cheek and his hands busy with file cards and schedules. The travel business, as my father later explained to me, was about creating connections, a bridge of good faith that spanned both miles and bureaucracies, safely delivering a Mrs. Seligman of Côte-des-Neiges Street, first to the shops of London and Paris and finally to a happy reunion with her husband waiting in Rome.

"Absolutely, Mrs. Seligman," my father chanted into the telephone while he jotted notes on file cards. "May 15th departure...."

Directories consulted. Schedules and prices compared. Calls to the airline and steamship company to double-check. Flights booked. Dates changed. Connections adjusted. More calls to Mrs. Seligman and the airline. Requests made for a dietetic meal of cottage cheese and fruit, also for a seat beside the wing so that she would not see the ground whirl away during takeoff. Deposits delivered. Passport application filed. Hotel in London cabled. Collect call from Rome accepted. Pension in Paris confirmed. Porter promised. Airline ticket collected (a run 10 blocks down Park Avenue and St. Catherine Street to the company's office on Beaver Hall Hill.)

One more phone call, person-to-person from a growly Mr. Seligman in Naples.

"Tell her not to come. She is *not* to come."

Reservations, connections, confirmations, deposits, applications — the bridge collapsed. Everything, including my father's meagre commission, aborted.

My father could only sigh, replace the receiver in its cradle, tear up the Seligman cards, busy himself with another file and wait for the phone to ring again.

My mother could not, at first, understand why she found our street so forbidding. Eventually, she realized it was the lack of trees. There were only saplings on small squares of lawn in front of each house, weak, pathetic things dwarfed by the massive brick behind and the wide road in front. The houses had a sameness to them, like soldiers' tombstones, but it was the treelessness that was most disturbing. It was worst on bright May days that exposed the graceless lines of unadorned doorways and windows and monotonous brick.

Having discovered a fact, she felt compelled to state it out loud. "This is Canada," she said to my father. "Wild forest everywhere, but on our street, only twigs."

His voice poured over her like coarse sand. "You don't like it here, go back. I'll buy you a ticket. Sea or air, your choice."

"Why do you hate me? What have I done to you?"

He turned and pulled away. There he lay, on his side of the bed, rigid and self-contained, and she knew he would be able to lie like that, neat as a board, without flinging a careless arm or leg toward her, all night long. To throw her arms around him now would be to smash like an egg against concrete. Still, she couldn't bring herself to move to the couch. She hung onto the bedsheets, twisting and twisting the sweat-dampened cloth in her hands.

One of the first things that my father bought with the few dollars he managed to set aside, after all the weekly and monthly expenses had been paid, was a vacuum cleaner. Riding the streetcar home that evening, he stood with one proud arm draped around a tall cardboard box stamped: MORGAN'S DEPARTMENT STORE. Canister, hoses, attachments and cord emerged from the box while my mother watched from the doorway of the living room.

"I don't need this thing," she said.

"It will make your life easier. Look." He plugged the vacuum cleaner in, scattered some shreds of toilet paper on the carpet and proceeded to demonstrate, just as the sales-man had. The motor still whining, he offered the hose to my mother. She shuffled across the carpet slowly, reached out her hand. *Crack!* A shock. Or so she said. Then the sucking mouth of the hose stuck to the carpet.

"Glide the hose. Don't rub. Don't drag so hard."

My mother jerked forward and the canister flipped over on its back, the motor releasing a high-pitched scream of alarm.

"You'll get used to it," he said. But except when my father took it out on Saturdays, the vacuum cleaner stood, abandoned, in the closet.

My mother worked. She tackled the kitchen floor with a string mop and a pail of sudsy water. She went at the linoleum as she had never done in Jerusalem, with a violent energy. She dipped, wrung, slapped the mop around and scrubbed some more, sending streams of grey water into the cracks of the flooring and under the cabinets to swell the crumbs and lumps that had collected there. She hoisted the metal pail, marched it to the toilet and tipped it in, listening with satisfaction to the splash and digestive gurgle. On her knees, leaning over the bathtub, she scrubbed the bedsheets between her knuckles. She rubbed, squeezed, twisted, wrung, then heaved the washtub to her hip and marched it to the clothesline.

She attacked the living room carpet, the only one in the house, first with a stiff brush, then with a damp cloth, dabbing and picking at the lint. She would have preferred to drag the carpet to the balcony railing and beat the dust out with a stick — heavy work and dirty, but effective. But people didn't do that in Canada. Could she imagine the names we'd get called, my father said, if the neighbours saw clouds of dust flying around their windows and clotheslines, let alone what the landlord would say?

My father noticed lint on the living room carpet and, worse, crumbs, shreds of vegetables and indefinable grime peeking out from under the kitchen cabinets. In Jerusalem, unwiped crumbs had produced an instant parade of red ants pouring out of a crack in the wall. Also cockroaches. He never got used to them. He remembered his nausea, stumbling into the kitchen for a glass of water at night and finding the scrabbling bodies, the evil shine of their brown-black shells in the electric light. Here, dirt had less drastic consequences. Maybe that was why she let it pile up. But no, he knew it was not deliberate. She was like a dreamy, awkward child, mooning about, unable to focus on things right in front of her nose. He knew better than to complain. But one day, while she was out of the room, he took a broom to the litter under the kitchen cabinets. He saw then he should have waited until she was out of the house altogether. She stormed into the kitchen like a maddened hen.

"What are you doing? What are you trying to prove?"

"I'm helping you. Is that a crime?"

"I've already swept."

"Well, you missed a bit." He pointed with the dustpan at the spot he'd been working on. He spoke in the most innocent, good-natured tone he could muster, but a guilty smile crept over his face. There was something else he wanted to say and now he'd forgotten. How could she make him feel guilty for *sweeping*?

"You try to humiliate me. You want to tramp me down into the mud."

In her eyes, a poison was rising, a fevered glaze. She swallowed, took a deep breath and hurled names at him in a rage — old woman, scorpion, snake — working herself up. Her voice rose higher, the glaze in her eyes grew thicker. Any moment, she would be over the edge, beyond reason. He searched for calm words but found none. Neither could he erase his grin.

"So? Better a scorpion in the kitchen than cockroaches, don't you think?"

Her mouth fell open. He pointed under the cabinets.

"Soon the cockroaches will come to dinner, just like old times."

She flailed her fists, chasing him around the kitchen. He dodged her, his arms shielding his face in defence.

"Set the table for them," he giggled between his fingers. "These honoured guests."

She slumped to the floor and cried: silent, spasmodic sobs; then bawling; and finally screaming between clenched teeth, shrill and fiendish. She bit at her arm, dug into her legs with her nails. Red welts and scratches blistered her skin and made his stomach lurch. His hands flew up to his eyes. A moment later he found what he'd been looking for: his anger – *he* was the one who was wounded.

"Quiet. Get a hold of yourself." He stooped over her, grabbed her hands in a vise grip. "Remember the children, for godsakes."

I was in my bed, in the little room far away at the back of the apartment, but I'd been wakened by less before.

"I forbid this behaviour." He shook her until her cries subsided into a quiet keening. She rocked from side to side, head on her knees. Sickened, his own knees weak, he loosened his grip and stood up. When she finally looked up, he was gone.

On his way to the bathroom to get ready for bed, my father noticed the back door ajar. He was about to lock it when the rattle of metal above his head caught his attention. He stepped onto the fire escape landing and his breath froze in his throat. Someone was climbing up to the roof on the short ladder that hung over the courtyard — my mother, in her bare feet and nightgown. To get onto the ladder, she would have had to clamber onto the narrow railing that surrounded our landing, then step sideways to the first rung. Now she was hoisting herself upward with unhurried, deliberate motions while my father watched in silence. In a moment she was on the roof, looking down the long chute of brick into the gloom below. A bathroom light was on, illuminating a sharp elbow of railing on the second floor, but beyond that it was all black.

My father's voice finally came unstuck. "What are you doing?" he said softly, afraid to startle her. She didn't seem to hear. She stood there hugging herself, looking downward while her nightgown fluttered against her legs in the wind. Although it was May, it was a frosty night, damp and windy. My father, dressed only in his undershirt and shorts, could sense, though he couldn't see, a thick bank of clouds rolling across the sky.

He cleared his throat. "Hannah, get down from there."

She swayed a little, arms tight to her chest. "Hannah, please."

She didn't lift her head. In his mind he went over the steps he had to take: a swift and noiseless leap up the ladder, a firm grab around the waist. Once he had her, he'd figure out how to get her down.

Apparently, at that moment, I began to cry. The sound of my wailing, thin and distant, drifted up the corridor and out the open back door. My mother looked around, startled and anxious.

"Go to her," she whispered.

"You go."

I continued to cry, frightened more than anything, perhaps, by the dead quiet that lay between my parents' room and myself. No radio tunes or voices or the clump of feet.

My mother crouched and put her bare feet back on the rungs. But, halfway down she realized what she was doing, where she was. She was suspended over nothingness, a chasm as vast and deep as the world itself, with the power to annihilate her. Cold metal rungs dampened under her grip.

"Come down," she heard my father say. From the corner of her eye she saw the white of his undershirt below her on the landing. She couldn't move. She couldn't breathe. To loosen a muscle meant to lose hold. Her back bent double and aching, her fingers locked to metal, she remained in a crouch as the ladder trembled against brick.

"Come on, just a few more steps," my father pleaded.

I continued to howl, louder and angrier. I was accustomed to someone coming right away. Most likely I wanted to run to them, but I was afraid of the pool of darkness around me, the stillness that lay thick and heavy in the rooms beyond.

"Take it easy. Don't panic," my mother heard my father say from a great distance. He moved into her line of vision and she saw with startling clarity how long and skinny his legs looked sticking out of his undershorts. Stork legs. She had a wild thought. "When this is over, I'll remember his legs and laugh."

A yank, a wrenching of such force came now, she could not resist. Her hands loosened, her arms flew out into the empty air. Her body, stone heavy, crashed on top of him and on top of the metal garbage bin, which flew off the landing, first the lid, then the rest of it, bouncing down three flights. Beneath her, his arms both clung to and lay pinned against her waist. His foot lay twisted under the railing. Slowly she rolled off him. They both sat up, stunned. He had a split lip and a sprained ankle; she, long gashes on her face where it had grazed against brick, massive bruises on one arm and an egg-size lump forming on her forehead.

Hearing the merry clang of the trash can, the sound of doors and windows opening and voices in the courtyard, I immediately stopped my crying. Calm and attentive, I waited for them to come.

Air and Earth

Rachel dips her foot in and out of the pool of sunlight on the wall above her bed and wonders what to do. It's Saturday morning, a shining day and a thousand green hands wave from the maple tree outside. She could join her mother on the long walk to the Steinbergs store or take her chances in the laneway, which might be full of kids later on, the scuffle of feet chasing rubber balls. But what if everyone's away on errands or holed up with Saturday-morning cartoons?

There's no point in trying to tag along with her brother Avi. She'd love to sit with him in a ditch near Dorval Airport, just once, watching planes take off and land while he calls out their names above the roar of the engines. But it's too far; she's not allowed.

The door swings open and her mother bursts in, in bare feet and nightgown, making a beeline for the balcony that opens off Rachel's room. Hannah grabs the handle of the balcony door and yanks. The glass panes rattle. Gusts of cool summer breeze blow through the room. Hands on the railing, Hannah sucks in early-morning air, the only air, she says, that's clean. It's not yet blown out of other people's mouths or dirtied by the traffic.

In another moment she's at Rachel's bedside.

"Where's my kiss," she whispers, her voice choked.

Her red-rimmed, watery eyes mean she's spent the last half hour locked up in the bathroom with the taps on full blast. One nasty word could send her back in there. Still, Rachel's mind is made up. The laneway beckons. A fast, wild game of handball is what she wants. She plants a smack on her mother's cheek, wriggles back against the wall and folds her arms across her chest.

"I'm going out to play. I'm not coming shopping."

"You don't want to come with me?" Her mother's eyes dart back and forth. She sinks down onto the edge of the bed, leans forward, shoulders hunched. After a long moment, her head snaps up. She smiles, though her eyes are still wet.

"Of course you're coming. It will do you good, a proper walk in the fresh air. The last time I came home to find you howling under my bedcovers."

This was true. Rachel had found no one to play with, returned home to the empty apartment where the silence in each room mocked her, like a friend turned mean. Each piece of furniture had become a stranger — couch, dining room table, the radio on her parents' dresser, the cuckoo clock with its dull brass pendulum. She whimpered into the pillows on her parents' bed, then advanced to full-throated wailing. She bawled into the empty grey space under the bedspread until Hannah walked in with her bulging shopping bags. Then, she threw herself against her mother's soft belly. Ashamed yet relieved, Rachel promised herself that it would never happen again.

"I'll be OK this time, don't worry." Rachel is anxious to be dressed and outside, away from the smell of the sleep-rumpled bed. No sound comes from Avi's room next door.

Maybe he's already pedalling his way across town to the airport, his eyes peeled for a streak of silver in the sky.

"Your father...," Hannah starts, looks away. "Your father will be working late," Rachel remembers now, dimly as in a dream, the sounds of voices earlier, one low, measured, steady as a saw rasping into wood, the other shrill and fluttering. Rachel sees the stiffness in her mother's back, how she needs a hand to touch and stroke her right in the dip where neck meets shoulders.

"I'll help you unpack the groceries when you get home. I'll play on the street so I see you coming."

But Hannah doesn't answer. She sits with legs crossed, hands laced around her thick knee, rocking slightly. Pale skin peeks from a gap in her nightgown where a button has come undone. All Hannah's dresses and nightgowns are the same style, with a long row of buttons up the front. She likes clothes she can slip in and out of without a struggle.

"When we lived in Jerusalem," she often says, "I wore a simple skirt and blouse and sandals and no one thought anything of it. Who had time or money for anything else?"

In clothing stores, when the salesladies try to show her something new, a dress with a gathered waist or a zipper up the back, Hannah's mouth twists.

"Oh, no, that's not for me," she says in a small, apologetic voice. But even her usual dresses don't work quite right for Hannah. A button, around the middle or near her knees, comes undone. A loop of hem hangs down. Rachel's father is forever pointing this out.

"There, there! Can't you see?" Ernst mutters as Hannah fumbles. "For godsakes, the way you run around."

The other mothers at Steinbergs look sideways at Hannah. She never curls her hair like they do; instead she keeps it short and straight with a part on one side. Rather than high heels, she wears white oxfords and socks. She speaks with an accent. "How much is ziss," she asks the vegetable man, making him smirk and Rachel walk away.

"I hate shopping," says Rachel, pressing closer to the wall.

She stares through the window's milky sheers to the side wall of the apartment building across from their own. It's a good wall for handball: a long expanse of brick with few windows to get in the way. Rachel's old rubber ball is cracked and pockmarked, its spongy insides exposed. It flies off at crazy angles when she smacks it against the brick with the palm of her hand. She longs for a new, smooth one that bounces straight up, high.

Hannah slumps, knuckles pressed against her cheek. Her back is arched, stiff, awkward. Rachel's stomach tightens. She wants to scream and flail her arms, but her hands do something quite different. They become like the white-gloved Mickey Mouse hands in the cartoon that detach from Mickey's body to play piano all by themselves. Her hands reach out, one rests on Hannah's shoulder, the other strokes the back of Hannah's head, tickling the greyish scalp under her thick black hair. She is amazed at what her fingertips know, the delicate movements they invent and the magic that flows through them. Her mother sighs between clenched teeth.

Now there's no longer any question of what to do. Rachel knows she will trot by her mother's side with a string bag in her hand, up the long street and through the woods behind the university. Certainty clamps down like a hand on Rachel's shoulder, brings with it a dull calm, a kind of relief.

ε

Avi is dressed, standing on the balcony, scanning the sky. In the distance, she hears the roar of an engine and a grey pencil shape appears above the roofs.

"TCA Super Constellation on its way to Winnipeg." Avi's voice purrs with certainty. It's impossible to tell if he's b.s.-ing, pretending to have X-ray vision. The grey shape passes over the far-off buildings, then thins and lightens to a silver streak.

"You can't see the name on that plane."

"Of course not. So what." His face is tilted away from her, but his eyes flick sideways. Triumphant accusations die in her throat. Her dumb-girl self is about to be exposed.

"I know it's a Super Connie by the three-pronged shape of the tail and the sound of its four engines. That's the plane TCA's using for long-haul flights. And it's 9:05," Avi says with a glance at his watch. "TCA Montreal to Winnipeg departs at nine."

Avi has memorized the schedules off the signboards at the airport. He can reel off the names — BOAC, Lufthansa, Swissair, Eastern — their departure times and arrivals, the number of miles they will travel to reach their destinations and how many horses it would take to pull them across the sky. He knows, too, what keeps an airplane from falling out of the sky, the invisible forces of air and earth.

Sometimes, when he squints at the sky and intones the names and numbers, he says, "I'm making an educated guess," but this is when Rachel is most impressed. It is what he becomes when he gazes upward, his eyes narrowed with concentration, his voice strong, deep, unstoppable, the whole world spinning, humming, ready for takeoff, inside him.

When it's time to leave, Hannah stands by the front door
with the handle of her purse between her teeth, both hands
deep in its belly. She's making sure she has everything —
keys, money, kerchief, string shopping bags, mailbox key.
"*Um Gotteswillen*," the mailbox key is missing. It should be
in the zippered side pocket, but it's not to be found. She
rushes back into the bedroom, rips open the top dresser
drawer, rummages among the underwear.

"I just had it a second ago," she wails.

The key is on the kitchen table, looped over the
saltshaker for safekeeping, Rachel knows this, but she
continues to linger by the door. The frenzy of departure
makes Rachel feel both giddy and nervous — like watching
a pie-throwing scene on *I Love Lucy*. She wants to laugh
out loud as she watches her mother tear at knots of
balled-up nylons. She also wants to flop in weariness onto
the hallway floor.

Hannah races down the corridor into the kitchen. A
yell of triumph. They're out the door, down the three
flights of stairs and into the lobby. They check the row of
metal mailboxes along the wall. No blue air letter from
England winks through the slats, nothing but boring
brown envelopes. They'd hoped for a letter from Edith,
who lives over the ocean in the land of Cadbury milk
chocolate and who tells funny stories about a cat named
Mr. McGregor.

"Maybe tomorrow," Hannah sighs, then hurries out into
the street. Halfway down the block, though, she stops dead,
gasps. Is the stove really off? The toaster unplugged, the

bathroom and kitchen-sink taps shut? She is only satisfied after Rachel runs back for a final, final check.

"Everything's fine!" Rachel shrieks from the steps of their building.

"Thank God. Thank God."

They walk forward together into the early summer breeze.

The Steinbergs on Côte-des-Neiges is about a mile from their house, a short ride by streetcar, but Hannah prefers to walk and it's not just to save money. Hannah hates everything fast and electric. The blue sparks that dance on the streetcar rod make her shiver and the rocking motion of the trolley makes her face get white and clammy.

"I should have been born in another time," she says. "In my mother's time. The world was so much nicer with horses and buggies."

Hannah can remember a fairy-tale life long ago. She had ridden, once, with her parents in a black coach over cobbled streets. And before electric lights, there were lanterns. A man came with a long pole to light the gas that hummed in the lamps near the schoolroom ceiling, the sound making Hannah so nice and sleepy.

Even better than riding coaches, Hannah says, is walking where you need to on your own two feet. This is one subject upon which her parents agree — the pleasures of walking. On fine Sundays, when Ernst doesn't have to work, the whole family sets out to cross Mount Royal and the Christian cemeteries to the lookout that hangs over the city like a balcony. Rachel loves it when the four of them go together. Four is the perfect number. Four wheels to a car. Four legs on a table. The number that holds things up.

The walk over the mountain, Ernst and Hannah say, is a real excursion, European-style, not the little circle around the block that Canadians call a walk. The green of Mount Royal with the spidery cross in the distance reminds them of the forests, castles and school outings back home. The whole class would take the tram to the end of the line and hike all day, drunk with fresh air and freedom. They wandered, but they weren't lost like Goldilocks in the forest. In Europe you could walk off in any direction and eventually end up in a village or a barnyard where a farmer's wife might offer you milk fresh from the cow. Try that in Canada, Ernst says, and you'd get stuck in the bush with a thousand blackflies up your nose. In Europe, there were "wandering songs" everyone sang, like Christmas carols, to get into the swing of forward motion.

Hannah begins humming to herself as she and Rachel walk together down the long sun-warmed street. Under her breath at first, she half whistles, half sings, until her voice, rich and low, wells up. *"Freut euch des Lebens."* Rejoice in life. Rachel chimes in here and there on the notes that are easy to reach. Since they are walking briskly they can do this — sing without being noticed by the woman in the yellow housecoat and pink sponge curlers who is sweeping her front steps or by the fat man with his feet up on the balcony railing. They pass by as if they are on a train.

"Tell the story about the time you ran away," Rachel says.

"Ran away?" Hannah looks down, puzzled.

"You know. When you ran away from home. Across the border. When you walked for three days by yourself."

"Oh, that. When I went to the training school. But I didn't run away, I just left. It was still easy to leave Germany then. I walked through the Riesengebirge, the mountains near our town, until I got to the Czech border. Someone had told me about a Herr and Frau Schatz who ran an agricultural school for young people, preparing them to be pioneers in Palestine. At first they didn't want to take me. There I was, scratched and dirty on Herr Schatz's front porch, and he stares at my swollen feet through his old-fashioned monocle and shakes his head, 'We need big strong boys here, not girls. You'd be devoured by the Palestine fevers in a week.' But we talk. He asks me about my town, my family, then suddenly he slaps his hand to his forehead. 'Your father's in the Lessing Lodge? Why didn't you say so?' And that was that. I was in."

"Why did you go alone? Why didn't Dad go with you?"

"But that was before I met your father. Don't you remember? I was on an excursion in the mountains with the youth group. Someone told me about the school, about learning to pitch hay and milk cows. I decided it was for me, decided to go right away. I left the next day from the youth hostel."

"But what did your father say? Did he just let you go?" Walking away without baggage or goodbyes, the thought of it is too wonderful, yet Hannah tells the story as if it were little more than a simple and ordinary truth. Rachel remembers the time when she stayed out after dusk in the park nearby. The house was in an uproar when she came home. Her parents had called the police.

"Oh, I must have written...I think my father and your aunt Edith were also packing up. Those were times when everyone was on the move." Hannah shakes her head.

Rachel could listen to this story again and again — a story about a girl who turned her mind inside out like a pillowcase, shook out any last-minute worries and filled herself with certainty and purpose. What did she eat? Where did she sleep? Were Hitler's men hiding in the bushes? Rachel wants to know more, but Hannah never seems to remember these details. She shakes her head again. So long ago. Instead her mother talks about the joy of walking in the mountains in a time before highways: the pine-scented wind, the distant cowbells, the cathedral of trees, the holy stillness of the woods.

They arrive at a busy corner. The light is changing from green to yellow. Hannah grabs Rachel's hand in a tight grip although they've both already come to a full stop. As the cars roll by, Hannah tells Rachel to take shallow breaths, so that the stink of the car exhaust doesn't enter her lungs.

"Can you believe it?" Hannah says. "I am still here, on this earth, and you are here, and your brother too, because my father was in the same lodge as Herr Schatz."

Her voice, which has been a light singsong, as if she were reading a fairy tale, now trails off into a mutter. She is far away in the time before Rachel was born. That time is like a puzzle whose pieces fit together with a snap. There was a war. Hitler came like Pharaoh to kill all the Jews, but a few Jews escaped over the sea and rebuilt their country from nothing. They came out of their crowded alleys into the brilliant light of the Land. They threw away their canes and monocles, dug their hands into the hot sand, and flowers burst forth where their fingers had ploughed. Many were killed, but some were saved. The chosen.

But other times it's as if pieces from a completely different puzzle are mixed with this one so nothing fits, just patches of colour without shape.

Rachel doesn't know what a lodge is. She suspects she still wouldn't understand the story if she did. Nor can she quite believe her mother would walk through the mountains all alone, although she can see, quite clearly, a grown-up girl, slim and tanned, with muscled arms and sturdy legs: the girl on the first page of the photo album, looking up in surprise. Oh, yes, she can see this girl with her bundle over her shoulder, one arm swinging free. She strides up a steep path and Rachel strides with her, bold and confident. They rise to the top of the mountain, while in the valley far below a wall of water crashes upon Hitler's army. All his men and chariots are drowned in the sea.

They emerge from Steinbergs weighted down by bags of groceries. Hannah clutches the ones with the heavy stuff — sacks of potatoes, onions, cans of Spam, the gallon jug of Javex, Old Dutch cleanser. Rachel twirls the bag that holds bread and oatmeal and, although it's not heavy now, she knows it will become so.

"Let's take the streetcar, Mama, just this time." Hannah watches as the streetcar swings around the corner and lumbers toward them. It is crammed with Saturday shoppers whose heads roll forward and back with the motion of the car. The ride would deliver them to their doorstep in five minutes flat. Rachel would have new transfers to add to her collection, a shoeboxful that once belonged to Avi before he gave up on streetcars to concentrate on planes.

"You'll only get sick. It's not so far to walk," Hannah says.

The streetcar pulls away in a shower of blue sparks. The street it leaves behind is long and straight, a monotony of buildings, an endless line of telephone poles and sidewalk slabs. Her legs become stiff and stubborn. They will never get her home.

"Look, let's pretend we only have to go to the next telephone pole," says Hannah. "Come, it's not so far."

In a few steps they are at the pole.

"Now just to the next one," Hannah says.

"To the next one," Rachel yells, dashing forward.

One by one, poles come forward to meet them, poles are left behind. They are walking again with feet that know their business. Walking, like breathing, in a rhythm that takes over. One, two, one, two.

When they pass by the Catholic cemetery, Rachel and Hannah turn onto the shortcut, a path that winds through woods, sumac groves and a field of hip-high weeds where bees buzz and butterflies flit. On one side, tractors plough a new road. The earth beneath their tracks becomes mashed and raw.

The sky is a vast expanse of watery blue, so far away that Rachel can't imagine how airplanes reach it so quickly. A few moments and a plane is transformed from a lumbering metal elephant into a silver speck. High above now, a pinpoint of light pierces the blue, pulling behind it a long thread of white cloud. She blinks. The white thread breaks up into ragged patches like pieces of couch stuffing. Avi could connect these lines to form a continuous path stretching across the ocean to a place called London or Paris. He could find his way in that endless blue. Rachel can't ever imagine being able to distinguish the voice of one engine from another or looking up at a pinpoint of light and calling it by name, like an old friend.

A small cry cuts through the silence, stopping Rachel in her tracks. Hannah is a short way back on the path, stock-still, bent over, the grocery bags scattered around her. Mouth open, she is peering into a tangle of leaves. Rachel can't see anything at first except a bumblebee that knocks against Hannah's hip and zigzags away.

"There. Right there."

On a leathery leaf sits a black-and-orange butterfly. It's the same as dozens of others that Rachel has seen flitting in the field, except this one has come to rest, its wings spread open, quivering ever so slightly.

"Do you see? So beautiful," Hannah whispers, squeezing her hands together. Rachel sees its delicate pattern of segments and dots, the glow of orange against velvet black. But there is too much of something in Hannah's face. And the grocery bags shouldn't be lying like that, limp and exposed, so that anyone passing by could see their things — the dented tins for five cents off, the Javex that Hannah uses for scrubbing the toilet.

Rachel tugs at her mother's sleeve, but Hannah doesn't seem to hear. The back of her neck is red and sweaty beneath the straight line of her black hair. The cardigan tied by the arms around her waist and swaddling her broad hips is bunched with burrs.

If boys from Rachel's school were to come upon them now, Hannah wouldn't notice until they were all around her, sticking their tongues out the sides of their mouths and making circling motions with their fingers by their temples.

Crazy. Crazy. Rachel feels the nasty word form on her lips. She wants to punch her mother's heaving breast. She wants to fly down the path and never look back. But the look on Hannah's face is breathless wonder, almost like pain, an unbearable joy. Rachel looks down, yet still sees her mother's parted lips and burning eyes. She takes hold of Hannah's hand, the thick, swollen fingers with purple lines across the knuckles where the string bag has cut them. She feels the coolness of her own hand soothe the sweaty heat, her mother's answering squeeze, the strong, enveloping grip.

"Come on, Mama," she says. "Let's go."

Who You Are

*T*he Hebrew script is barbed wire on the page: dense and deadly, row upon row of tangled letters with lacerating points. It surrounds Avi, threatens to cut him to pieces. He tries to focus and separate the tangle. An *aleph*, a *lamed*, a *hey*...slowly the word reveals itself, *"Elohim,"* one of the names, but not *the* name of God, and then it sinks again into the confusion of jagged edges. Avi leans over the table, stares down at the page until the black daggers dissolve into a blur of wandering flies.

And this is the *easy* stuff, Weissbloom, his tutor, has told him. Much harder texts are to come, texts in which words run together in endless chains with no spaces between them and a blizzard of squiggles form musical notations. Even if he could read the words, it would not be good enough. You have to chant for your bar mitzvah, each quaver of the voice preordained. You have to moan out the words in an old-man singsong that gives Avi the creeps.

Across the dining room table Avi's father whispers under his breath, *siebenunddriessig, neunundzwanzig vierzig,* as he jots down figures in his notepad. On one side of the page is the tower of monthly expenses: rent — $85, groceries — $25, shoes for Rachel — $2.88 (from Larry's Warehouse clearance sale). Modest sums by themselves, but heaped one atop the other, they make a crushing pile. Electricity,

GABRIELLA GOLIGER

telephone, streetcar fare, tutoring for Avi, et cetera, et cetera. Somewhere in the et cetera, Avi hopes, is a small amount set aside for his birthday present, which, if there were any justice in the world, would be a new Raleigh three-speed bicycle, but Avi will settle for a $10-bill.

With each entry, Ernst's brow furrows deeper, his face sags further. He jots, crosses out, revises, tots up again, shakes his head and pushes his fingers through the stiff grey-black hair above his temples. The left-hand column has to add up to the single figure on the right side of the page — Ernst Birnbaum's estimated salary. The amount varies from month to month, depending on commissions, but it doesn't usually rise above $150. About a third of what his father's most important client, Hendelman the scrap-metal dealer, makes. About a hundredth of what Avi intends to make when he grows up.

Avi would gladly help bring the left-hand column down a peg or two.

"That tutor costs a lot, eh, Dad?"

Ernst's ballpoint pen pauses in the air, but his head stays bent over the notebook.

"If I didn't have to take lessons...."

"Just hurry up and finish. You have to leave in half an hour."

"But it's a waste of money, the whole thing."

His father raises his head, finally, and his eyes, behind thick glasses, are cool, measuring, unimpressed. He appears to read Avi's thoughts only to conclude they don't amount to much. Pots rattle in the kitchen where Avi's mother is preparing the Sunday dinner of roast chicken and potatoes. From outside comes the deep-voiced drone of a DC-3, a familiar, throaty growl that calls Avi to the window. He has to wrap his sweaty feet around the chair legs to keep himself from jumping up.

It's hotter than usual for the end of May. A bit of dandelion fluff wafts into the room. In his damp basement apartment on St. Bernard Street, Weissbloom, the cockroach, is waiting. There is no justice in the world. Avi allows himself the pleasure of a long, loud moan.

The pen raps sharply against the edge of the table.

"You'll get through this," his father says. "Just apply yourself."

Apply what? Avi wishes he could wrench loose the cold, rusted machinery of books, but words lie inert on the page and he hovers above them panicked and useless. At school, his homeroom teacher, Mr. Murray, taps the wooden pointer smartly against the back of Avi's head and bellows, "Give me an example of the ablative absolute. I'm waiting, Birnbaum. Anything in there?"

A sneer lurks in Murray's voice, a private sneer just for Avi.

"You Jew boys are supposed to be so smart," the sneer says. "Well, Birnbaum, how come *you're* such a moron?"

His report cards are wastelands of "F"s. The "F," which stands for "fair", but really means "foul", stamps disappointment into his father's eyes.

"School is an opportunity," Ernst intones. "When I was a bit older than you, I had to leave school to work. I've regretted it my whole life."

But what baffles Ernst even more than the poor report cards is Avi's indifference to books. How can a son of his not love books?

"When I was your age I read everything I could get my hands on. Karl May, Jules Verne."

Avi can't explain how the written word stops his fluttering mind in midflight and drags it down. He needs a moving target to focus on — a reeling, rollicking world, the patterns of the stars. He can read the sky for constellations, knows the sizes and distances of planets. This, at least, impresses his father.

It was Ernst who first got Avi to see the imaginary lines connecting the bright points above them as they stood, shoulder to shoulder, on the balcony on moonless nights. Now, Avi recognizes more stars than his father and can gaze at them longer than Ernst, who has to remove his glasses and rub his eyes after a while. Avi recites statistics. Regulus is 85 light years away. Arcturus is bigger than, but not as hot as, our sun. A beam of light travels from Earth to the moon in just over a second. Each fact is a rocket soaring into space. Ernst nods, smiles, exclaims with wonder. But few nights are dark or clear enough for stargazing. And sometimes, in the midst of the recitations, Ernst stops listening, leans forward against the railing and sighs.

"The Earth is a speck. We are nothing," says Ernst in a bewildered way that brings a sudden ache to Avi's chest.

Avi slams shut his Hebrew prayer book and decides to practise instead the blessings that Weissbloom has written out for him in English letters. *"Baruch atah adonai...."*

He covers his ears with his hands and shakes back and forth. This is better. He slides off the chair, falls with a thud onto the carpet, arms wrapped around his head, a wounded soldier dodging enemy fire. He chants louder, his voice shoots into the air, retaliates.

"Are you a lunatic?" His father's voice is dry, sarcastic, weary.

"I'm praying. I'm learning to pray like a Jew."

Avi sits up, elbows on knees, rocks back and forth and chants through his nose, whining out the words. *"Baruuuch, ataah, adonoy, yoy, yoy, yoy."*

Rachel pokes her head around the doorway and collapses, shrieking, onto the floor. Avi glances up through his fingers at his father and a prayer flies up, unbidden. Let his father be filled with wrath. Let him rain down fire and brimstone. Let him deem his son unworthy of a bar mitzvah. Let him cancel the whole sorry affair.

The telephone rings. Ernst's head jerks up in surprise and Avi's mother pads from the kitchen into the hall. "It's for you," she says to Ernst, pressing her lips together, her face dark with reproach. "Can't they leave you alone on Sunday?"

Ernst rushes into the hall. His voice, normally low and even, becomes high and fluttery.

"Mr. Hendelman, how nice to hear from you," he sings. "Is that so? How terrible. Yes, of course. No, no. No trouble."

The phone clatters in its cradle, Ernst murmurs something in the kitchen and a pot slams down on the counter.

"Du lieber Gott. It's Sunday. It's outrageous. What am I supposed to do with dinner?"

"Don't worry, I'll be back in time for lunch," he mumbles and rushes into the bedroom, emerging a moment later, buttoning up a fresh white shirt.

"Come on, come on," he calls to Avi. "I'm going with you downtown. I have some work to do at the office."

His fingers stop suddenly in midair and he looks down at his botched handiwork, the end button left without a buttonhole, the whole row out of alignment. With a sigh he begins again, squeezing his eyes shut for a moment as if the morning sunlight pouring in through the dining room window blinds him.

Ernst strides toward the streetcar stop with firm, urgent steps, a man with no time to waste, while Avi hangs back, hands in his pockets. Mrs. Couette, in curlers and bathrobe, is smoking on her balcony. A knot of little kids is crouched on the curb, banging rocks against caps that *crack, crack* in the air. Mrs. Couette's bathrobe is tied tight for a change and she stands as still as the railing she leans on, so there's none of that wonderful commotion that he sometimes spies and that makes him thrill with joy and disgust. He wheels around. He scans the street for cars. A white De Soto sits on the corner beside the drugstore, its motor running. A dusty old Edsel chugs by. What he'd really like to see is the car in the Harold Cummings ad — a two-toned, yellow-and-white Buick convertible with a V-8 engine, automatic transmission, power steering, whitewall tires. It would slip down the street. It would glide on a stream of air.

"Hurry up," Ernst calls over his shoulder.

"What for?" says Avi, gesturing toward the empty street, no streetcar in sight. They might be waiting for ages.

"Why do you dawdle?" Ernst calls back and continues his march to the corner, driven, as always, by some inner clock. His hurrying footsteps say nothing can be trusted to happen when it's supposed to. You have to be too early to avoid being too late. The more his father rushes, the more Avi's pace slows. The best part of a streetcar ride is leaping over the folding steps and through slamming doors at the last minute.

A hand tugs his shirtsleeve. Billy McDougall looks up at him, fatso Billy, freckles afloat on his sweaty but eager face.

"Ya have any golf balls?" Billy pipes.

As a matter of fact, Avi has. He always keeps a few in his schoolbag in case of an opportunity for a quick sale, a nickel a piece. Billy stares at him, mouth slightly open, pondering his options. He hauls five pennies out of his pocket and the exchange is made. Billy charges down the street toward his friends, the battered golf ball clutched in his fist.

Avi collects discarded golf balls whenever he's invited to work as a caddy for Mr. Hendelman. He gets 25 cents for wheeling clubs and chasing strays across the smooth grass, then doubles his money with sales to kids who have discovered the exciting combination of golf balls and streetcar wheels.

Number 23 finally swings into view several blocks away. Avi checks his watch and tries to calculate the speed of its approach by a quick estimate of distance and the movement of the second hand. His father flaps his hand and glares in Avi's direction.

Billy runs into the middle of the street and places his prize onto one of the tracks so that the streetcar wheels can roll over and crack the dense white golf ball shell.

Clang! Clang! Clang! Avi flies toward the corner and leaps aboard, whacking his forehead against his father's shoulder blade. From the window he watches the kids chase the scalped and spinning ball down the gutter. The lucky one who retrieves it will sit on the curb and spend a happy half hour unravelling the golf ball's exposed guts — yards of tightly wound elastic that yield to the pluck of fingers and that end up as a soft brown nest of tangles on the sidewalk. The kids have not yet tired of the game, but Avi is careful not to glut this fragile market. He never sells more than a few balls at a time.

The streetcar is almost empty and eerily quiet. A man a few seats up slumps over the top of the seat in front of him, head buried in his arms. A couple of ladies in hats and half veils sit farther down the aisle. All Avi can see of their faces are their pinched mouths. He feels the holiday that is not a holiday press down on his head. For once he's not in the mood to swing from the leather straps on the ceiling. His father in jacket, white shirt and tie, sits neat and composed and unperturbed by the oppressive silence around them. Avi flings his arms onto the back of the empty seat in front of him, flops his head upon them and finds himself staring at a familiar spidery figure. Someone's scratched a swastika into the varnished wood beneath the window. A small one, hardly noticeable. With the tip of his key, Avi scratches two more twisting legs and the figure is gone, blended with all the other dents and scribbles in the wood.

A bar mitzvah won't make Murray stop sneering. A bar mitzvah didn't save his father from the Germans. What saved his father was knowing when and how to get out.

Avi asks the question that wells up inside him almost daily and keeps getting beaten down or shunted aside.

"Why do I have to have a bar mitzvah?" he says, directing his words at a blotch of what looks like spit on the window. "I could be caddying right now. I could be earning my keep."

"All Jewish boys have bar mitzvahs."

"But what for? Give me one reason."

"I hated the lessons as much as you do."

"But your father was religious. We're not."

The family lights candles at Hanukkah and eats a festive meal at Passover, but on the Day of Atonement the four of them steal away from the city on an early-morning train. They travel north to St. Eustache-on-the-Lake with picnic sandwiches and a Thermos of tea discreetly packed into an old cloth bag. They spread out their feast on a beach they have all to themselves; gone are the rows of oiled sunbathers who covered almost every inch of available sand during the summer. Huddled together under a high, clear October sky, they watch wavelets dance against the shore. With embarrassed grins, his parents speculate about what it's like back in the city — people crammed together in a stuffy synagogue, twitching in their stiff and itchy holiday best, the mutter and wail of prayers. After lunch he and his father and Rachel skip stones on the rough surface of the water, exulting in their loose and lonely joy.

"It's not a matter of religion," Ernst says. "It's so you know who you are."

There it is again. Avi's father's final position. He brings it forward, places it in the air between them with grim triumph. The argument spins round on itself and leads nowhere, but beats Avi down with its perplexing force. Avi has played a variation of the debate with Rachel, to torment her, but also curious to see how it works.

"Do you know who you are?" he asked.

"I'm Rachel," she said, staring back, an edge of irritation already in her voice.

"How do you know that?"

"Because...because, that's what Mum and Dad called me."

"And if they called you something else, would you *be* someone else?"

"I'd be me," she screamed and hurled herself, fists thrashing, at his chest, before he could ask the clincher. "And who are you?"

Avi glances at his father and comes to the one conclusion that is most preposterous of all. His father has no reason to insist on the bar mitzvah. This cool, sensible man, this man of reason, has no reason. Why else would he clamp his jaws together and refuse to talk about it any more?

Before they began stargazing together, Avi used to think that his father believed in *something*. He saw him late one night steal quietly onto the balcony and stare at the dark sky. What else could he be doing but begging God to make the figures on the left side of the page bow down to the sum on the right? Watching from behind the curtain, Avi uttered his own fervent variations. The Raleigh three-speed, a television, a car. If you were going to ask, you may as well make it worthwhile.

All this was long ago. Now Avi knows that his father looks up at detached and distant stars and contemplates the riddle of the universe. The impossible possibility of unending space, the equally impossible thought of space coming to an end. Ernst mulls this over again and again without any hope of making sense of it.

The reason is a test, the reason is suffering through unreasonableness, the reason is the pleasure of beating your head against a wall.

The Hebrew lesson is a disaster, as usual. Weissbloom ushers Avi into the cramped apartment that he shares with three ancient creatures — two aunts and a parent, or two parents and an aunt, Avi can't remember which. He brings Avi into the kitchen and they sit down at the Arborite table amid smells of chicken fat, cabbage and some penetrating medicinal odour. One of the frail creatures shuffles forward with a pitcher of barely sweetened lemon water. She and Weissbloom chatter in Yiddish, which to Avi sounds like German spoken with your nostrils pinched together.

"So this is the *Yingle* who's becoming a man," says the aunt or mother, with a yellow-toothed grin.

Weissbloom repins his *yarmulke* to the wisps of orange hair raked across his balding head, rubs his hands together and says, in a voice full of hope, "Shall we begin?" Ten minutes later the *yarmulke* is listing, the strands of hair are damp with sweat, Weissbloom's forefinger is thumping the book, as if it were just a matter of looking down, "There! There!" to make the connection.

"No, no, no. *Holzkop*. Start again."

Locked together in a painful dance, teacher now pushing, now pulling, both stealing furtive glances at the wall clock, they teeter their way through the text. The second hand jerks in slow motion, the furniture creaks, sweat pricks Avi's neck, time kneels on his chest and refuses to budge. The smell of "F"s foul the air, the four walls close in, the room goes on forever. The last 15 minutes are a tightly wrapped elastic band that unravels, unravels, into a heap of brown tangles at his feet. Finally, the minute hand hits noon. Finally, it is time for his release. Weissbloom's voice softens again, regret and self-reproach welling up. He pats Avi's shoulder.

"You'll learn, don't worry," he says, unconvincingly.

Avi emerges from Weissbloom's dungeon onto the sunny sidewalk, muscles atwitch, mouth puckered with lemon water, furiously hungry. Why can't they ever have steak for dinner?

That's it. Finished. He'll never go back. His mind is made up.

His father can rage and storm, but he will stand firm, look his father straight in the eye with a calculating stare. He will take his father's measure and determine exactly how many minutes the storm will last until it's spent.

He enters the small doorway of his father's office on Park Avenue and takes the steps two at a time to the second floor, but a loud grating voice brings him to a halt.

Hendelman has not yet gone. A big, fleshy man with a tanned, bald head, he's planted in front of Avi's father's desk, tipping backward, leisurely, in the chair, a cigarette with a long snout of ash burning between his fingers.

"So what do you think they served that night for dinner?" Hendelman is saying. "Well, guess, just guess," he booms as Ernst shakes his head.

"Peking duck. Best I ever tasted. Have you ever tried Peking duck? No? Listen, go to Ruby Foo's, order it in advance. They have to get the spices from Chinatown, or maybe from China. But anyway, like I was saying, check for me if we can get a cabin at the back of the ship and if we stop over in Aruba...." And Hendelman talks, talks, talks, pauses to blow a thick stream of smoke into the air and talks some more while Ernst, hand cradling his cheek like someone who has a toothache, nods, scribbles notes and utters small appreciative sounds. Avi clears his throat and Hendelman turns his big bulk around in the chair, waves with two fingers and turns back.

"Let's go," Avi mouths to his father over Hendelman's naked head. Ernst raises his palm in a gesture of apology.

Several times Ernst opens his mouth to interject, but shuts it again as Hendelman drones on. On the wall behind his father's desk is a poster of an airplane's interior. A blond stewardess in a tight skirt bends down with a tray of drinks, a man smiles up and reaches toward her. "Fly TCA," says the poster. The folds of flesh on the back of Hendelman's neck settle down. Avi's stomach squirts acid.

Finally, Ernst manages to get Hendelman to his feet, but standing upright seems to give the fat man new energy and his lips flap with more anecdotes. Another eternity passes as he inches toward the door. The poison in Avi's chest boils over. His father is a weakling, a nothing, a nobody.

"How can you just sit there and let him walk all over you?"

Ernst shrugs and shakes his head. "You see what he's like once he gets talking...." Ernst shrugs again, turns to gather the papers on his desk, pulls a crumpled brown bag from a drawer and hands Avi a neat half sandwich. Rye bread with butter and cheese.

"Here, this will tide you over," he says, with a quiet look in his eyes, neither angry nor hurt, but sad, filled with a kind of stubborn dignity. He has the air of a man who could wait in the rain for hours. "It's useless to complain," say his eyes. "It's a waste of time."

Avi stuffs the bread into his mouth, surprised at how good it tastes, how his mouth waters and his legs, puny under the cloth of his pants, almost tremble with relief. Meanwhile his father empties his desk into a briefcase, cramming brochures, papers, file cards inside. The stoop of his shoulders is unbearable.

Avi longs to leap forward into the future, to be a man right now, a rich man, and not a *Yingle*. He would drive up to the front of the building in the two-toned Buick, throw open the door, invite his father to sink down into plush white leather. He'd press a button in the padded dash, make the roof fly open, gun the engine. "Ahh," his father would say, as the wind bathed his face. They would tear down the highway together, away from stupid file cards and niggling sums in a notebook. Away from the sickly lights of the city that pollute the pure black of the sky.

Maedele

On Tuesday and Thursday mornings Rachel's parents rise early to help deliver their daughter to Professor Blutstein, with whom she's having an illicit affair. Of course, they don't know that's what they're doing. They think they're helping her get a head start on her research at the library. She's off to work in the reserve section, she's told them, before other students have a chance to monopolize certain texts: the new *Encyclopedia Judaica*, Yiddish authors in translation, tales of the Hassidim. Rachel is both relieved and appalled at how easy it is to deceive her parents. Their daughter has developed a passion for Jewish studies and is on her way to becoming first in her class. Even her mother — a terrible snoop — appears to have only the most innocent of suspicions. Every now and then she wonders aloud if Rachel has a crush on some boy.

Deception comes easily, perhaps because the truth is so preposterous, so slippery. She's been singled out by a great Yiddish poet, a visiting professor from Jerusalem. She is having an affair with a married man old enough to be her father. She's receiving private lessons from a Holocaust survivor who saw babies butchered, who was buried under corpses, who hid in a pit for almost two years. She is dreaming a B-grade movie where too much happens, a calamity a minute.

She is dreaming corpses, she is falling into a pit, she is buried under a professor.

And now here comes Hannah into the kitchen, to prepare her daughter's lunch. Rachel protests, but to no avail. Lunch must be made by motherly hands, otherwise her daughter won't eat properly. Hannah's brow furrows with ancient anxieties that can only be soothed through the preparation of food. Rachel's father has a role to play, too. He insists on taking her. Why should she take the bus? He's driving downtown past the library anyway.

Hannah bustles, slices, spreads, wraps, hauls yet another item out of the fridge. Thick sardine sandwiches to nourish the brain; carrot sticks to strengthen the eyes; slices of homemade *Apfeltorte*, made Viennese-style with butter, almonds, eggs and cream. When she's finished the lunch, Hannah follows Rachel around, ostensibly to help her get ready, but really to postpone their separation. It will be a long, lonely day in the empty bungalow.

"Pink suits you," Hannah says. "A nice youthful colour."

Rachel turns this way and that in front of the mirror, examining herself in her embroidered blouse and cameo choker, wondering if she's got it right. She's striving for a combination of innocence and sophistication. The flower-child allure: loose blouse, tight jeans, granny shawl, subtle eyeliner, pale lipstick. A look to drive a professor wild. A look to make his wife go mad. But maybe the choker makes her neck seem too long.

She shakes the eyeliner bottle, applies the brush with an unsteady hand and ends up with black splotch at the corner of her eye and a wavy streak above her lashes.

"You don't need that stuff," says Hannah. "It's grotesque."

Rachel dabs her eye with Kleenex and begins again, more

successful this time, but, still, an awkward, girlish face looks back from the mirror. A pale unformed face, half hidden under a frizzy mop of hair. She moves on to eyelash curler, mascara, then the lipstick, a delicate shade called Cherry Blossom that looked good on the salesgirl at Ogilvie's.

A sly smile spreads across Hannah's lips. "So who is he?" she says.

Rachel freezes, holding the lipstick, a pink, exposed finger in the air.

"He?"

"The boy you're trying to impress?"

Rachel's shoulders relax a notch.

"You can tell your mother."

Rachel knows exactly the kind of boy Hannah has in mind. Tall, handsome, shy eyes, polite manner, blue blazer, gold buttons — an adolescent, Jewish version of Oscar Werner. Her mother's eyes gleam and her cheeks flush as if she's knocked back a stiff drink. And what would Hannah have to say about Professor Blutstein's craggy face against Rachel's belly?

"There's nothing to tell. Look, it's late." Rachel presses Cherry-Blossomed lips into a Kleenex, snaps the lipstick case shut and tosses it into her Mexican shoulder bag.

At 7:15, her father strides down the hall, briefcase in hand, face still damp from Gillette aftershave. He helps Rachel slip into her coat and fusses with the scarf around her neck. The first snow of the season is falling. She mustn't catch cold. Hannah stands at the door with the lunch bags, shoulders drooping, face upturned. She looks like a piece of luggage forgotten at a train station. Ernst pecks her quickly on the forehead, muttering a gruff goodbye. Now that the moment of escape is at hand, Rachel thaws. She leans forward to give her mother a hug but Hannah hangs on, collapses against Rachel as if she wants to sink into her daughter. Rachel jerks away and rushes out the door after her father.

They drive through grey, slushy streets in silence as the car heater puffs, the windshield wipers snap back and forth, sweeping away fat, wet flakes. The radio announcer rattles through a long list of accident reports and then, in a more dire tone, warns his listeners to stay away from the downtown core over the lunch hour. A huge anti-war protest is being planned, a protest that may become violent, he says, an edge of excitement in his voice.

"Terrible," her father mutters. "Where will it end?" Her father thinks the Americans are bungling the war in Vietnam. He also believes the protesters are pawns of the Soviets. This morning she doesn't feel like goading him with stories of atrocities. Instead, she wants to sink into her coat collar and a blur of daydreams that will prepare her for the rendezvous ahead. She needs calm. She needs languor. She needs her father to become a piece of unobtrusive, car-driving machinery, but he's unaware, as usual, of the message her averted face and hunched limbs convey.

"What are you working on now?" he asks, as they enter some stop-and-go traffic at Queen Mary and Côte-des-Neiges.

"I'm reading Martin Buber on the tales of the Hassidim. I'm writing a paper. It's for my Yiddish in Translation course." She hopes that these weighty titles will put him off.

"Ah. Yiddish." His head rocks back and forth, skeptical. "A funny language."

"You think so because you're such a *Yecke*." She meant to use a joking tone, but the word comes out harsh and stabbing.

"*Yecke!*" He rolls his eyes and emits a quick, forced laugh. "You *are* learning a lot."

Blutstein taught her the term *Yecke*, the German Jew: stiff, formal, even arrogant, hiding his Jewishness under a jacket and tie, embarrassed by the *shtetl* Jew's kaftan and beard. Her father's too self-effacing to be arrogant, she thinks, but he fits the bill in other ways. *The McGill Daily* would call him a model of bourgeois respectability. And both her parents look down their noses at Yiddish, bastardized German to their ears. To Rachel's, too, she has to admit. She tries to appreciate Blutstein's poetry, which he recites in class and which she can half understand. But she can't get beyond the outlandish sounds, the vowels stretched out like fat, wobbling bubbles in the air. A great language, yoking heaven and earth, the sacred texts and the common man, Blutstein tells her. But she is poisoned against it.

"The tales of the great Hassidic masters were told in Yiddish. The language of the people," she informs her father.

"Rabbinic tales," he grunts. "You find that interesting?" To him, Hassidic mysticism and garden-variety religion are one and the same, all hocus-pocus, medieval superstition.

"Very," she mumbles into her coat collar, wishing she could explain as Blutstein does. The tales seem both quaint and baffling until Blutstein reveals layers of meaning. How does he put it? A mysticism based not on mythology but on real events, the here and now and the very present then. Jewish memory goes back and back and back, to Sumer, Akkad, 3,000 years of Egypt, so that Greece and Rome are like yesterday to us, almost modern eras. The Jewish soul bears witness, suffers, has a destiny — to redeem the world by exposing the tyranny of empires and to reassert Jewish sovereignty, which is happening right now, this very moment. We live in wondrous times. But her version of Blutstein's lecture would be feeble and make him sound like a crazed romantic, or worse.

Mercifully, her father doesn't probe further. He shrugs, peers through his bifocals at the line of cars ahead, swings the wheel, and they dart forward into the faster lane of traffic, avoiding a stalled taxi. He beams at this small victory.

"So when is this paper due?" he asks.

"Next Friday."

"And you're making progress?"

"Yes."

"Good for you."

So pleased because she brings home good marks and pleases the professors, his studious daughter, never mind what she studies. Her oblivious father. He is silent again, concentrating on the road ahead. A song floats out from the car radio. "Let the sun shine in, let the sun shine in...." A song to make everyone feel better about the weather and the traffic and Vietnam.

Staring at a stubborn spot of ice that resists the battering of the windshield wipers, Rachel sinks down into her seat and drifts. She constructs a fantasy, beginning with a premise and adding details, a dab of colour here, another there, until the vision wraps her in its fuzzy warmth. The premise is that Mrs. Blutstein's gone to Paris. A gallery there is exhibiting her work. Meanwhile Blutstein waits for Rachel on the front steps of his apartment building. He paces with impatience, then catches sight of her youthful figure walking toward him.

His eyes glow when he sees her, graceful, nonchalant, her hair streaming in the wind (it has lengthened and straightened itself, by some miracle). He grabs her arm and guides her upstairs. No. He whistles for a cab, they go for a second breakfast at the Queen Elizabeth Hotel. No. They drive to a resort in the Laurentians. That's it, a resort in remote, snow-filled woods. He reaches for her hand across a dining room table and his eyes, brilliant with all that he knows and feels and has a hold on, these eyes burn toward her, reduce her to cinders.

As it was that first time. She had gone to his office late on a Friday afternoon, hardly expecting him to be there, conscious of the *clack* of her boots in the empty hallway. She'd been wrestling with a theme for her term paper and wanted help, but also — she sees it now — to catch a glimpse of the great Blutstein ensconced behind a desk. Would he become more ordinary, approachable and slightly fossilized, like the other professors? Or would he still radiate that compelling energy, as when he paced back and forth in the classroom, wresting truth from the air with tense, clenched hands? A short, stocky man with an oversized head and tiny feet, he should have looked cartoonish but didn't because of his restless, fluid movements and his breathless, excited speech. She was aware of listening, not to his words, but to the rise and fall of his voice, while she doodled a circus of amoebas in her notebook.

At her timid knock against the open office door, he leapt immediately from his chair and came around the front of the desk.

"It's you," he said, beaming with undisguised delight. "Come in, come in."

As if he'd been expecting her. She became flustered, blanked actually, and was unable to remember the introductory speech she'd been planning. He looked straight into her eyes with unsettling intelligence, a sly smile on his delicate lips, forming her with his gaze. A girl with designs. That's what he saw, that's what she was, she realized, with a shock of embarrassment and pleasure. She was wearing a miniskirt and mid-calf-length boots and clutched her coat and books to her chest, a gesture that put all the emphasis on her exposed, nyloned legs. She found herself smiling too. An absurd, complicit smile.

The moment lasted for an outrageous length of time. He was not afraid to let the room fill up with silence and with what seemed to be deepening shadows. The lights in the room were off, she realized, and dusk approaching. He continued to stare and smile and speak wordlessly with a lift of the eyebrow, a cock of the head, pantomiming wonder, invitation and also that delicious undercurrent of mischief.

She dropped her eyes and lifted them again, struggled to say something, while the chattering, doubting voice inside her subsided for once. Finally, she collapsed into nervous laughter, yet still he held her with his eyes. Had he mentioned right then that he was married, she would have stared at him in utter bewilderment, as if he'd asked her to solve a complex algebraic equation.

Mrs. Blutstein is not in Paris. The professor will be tucked away in his ninth-floor apartment. And Rachel's approach will be far from nonchalant. She will dart through alleys, hunch her shoulders, afraid of being seen by the wrong Blutstein. The Mrs. has cat's eyes, Rachel is convinced. Wide and penetrating and inescapable.

At the corner of McTavish and Sherbrooke, near the Redpath Library, father and daughter part ways, he to continue to the travel agency on Park Avenue, she to weave through the student ghetto until she comes to the street where the Blutsteins live. Unless, like today, she's early, which means she has time to poke about the campus and try to soothe her jangled nerves. In the lobby of the student union building, the bulletin board accosts her. Pay attention, it says.

Yellow Door Coffee House, Marxist-Leninists, ban the bomb, ride to New York, guitar for sale, Jewish students meeting, Christian Fellowship, we are, we are, we are the engineers, we can, we can, we can, demolish 30 beers, Marshall McLuhan in the Leacock Theatre (bring lunch), learn to meditate, boycott California grapes, fuck the fuzz, looking for crash pad, I have lost an earring shaped like a crescent moon, massacre at My Lai, stop the killing, march at noon.

She shifts from foot to foot. Should she go? She imagines the turbulent, confident crowd and their bold placards. "Burn pot, not people!" "End Canada's Complicity!" Stay out of trouble, her father would say. It's not your concern.

Blutstein disapproves too, but for different reasons. "Jews are on the front lines of every revolution that turns against them," he once said with a shrug, while his dismissive look told her that this business of marches was a petty distraction, a game.

She feels awkward in demonstrations, like someone who can't keep step in a dance. She watches her classmates — some of the girls especially — their practised, beatific smiles transformed into howls of fury directed at the government, the system. They can let go, yell, even shove and hurl stones. She can't get angry enough, or sure enough, to yell. The pictures and facts about tons of bombs dropped on villagers in rice paddies leave her numb or troubled, but don't give her that ironclad conviction you need for a demo. She grieves over the magazine picture of the huddled My Lai women about to be shot, a teenager in the centre with a grandmother's arms wrapped around her. At the same time, strangely, she cherishes this image because it's the only thing she can hold onto in all the news reports, speeches, posters. When Rachel tries to chant, all that comes out is a feeble squeak. Is Blutstein right? But surely he too has seen the photo of the women.

At a little after eight she is in the laneway beside the high-rise on Hutchison Street. She hesitates by the side door to the parking garage, looks over her shoulder. No one. She slips inside. The air smells of car exhaust and rotten eggs, but it is mercifully dark. The fire-escape door is propped open, left so by the careless janitor. If not, she'd have to back-track to the front entrance and run the risk of being seen. It's not just Mrs. Blutstein who worries her, it's anyone who might be in the lobby or elevator. She's afraid of suspicious glances, absurd, she knows, but a fear she can't shake.

She climbs up 126 stairs, arriving at the ninth floor breathless, armpits sweaty. She pokes her head into the hallway and looks for the newspaper on the mat in front of the door — their sign. If she sees it, all is well, she may tap at the door. If not, she must leave at once. Normally, by eight, Mrs. Blutstein's gone to the art college to teach her early-morning class.

All these details, and many others, have been worked out by Blutstein. There are signs, escape routes, contingency plans and, if worst comes to worst, a story to explain her presence in the apartment (she's late with a term paper, came personally to beg an extension). He's a master of subterfuge. Almost seems to relish it.

She smiles toward the peephole. The door opens a crack. She steps inside.

"*Maedele,*" he whispers in Yiddish as he pulls her toward him. More Yiddish endearments as he presses against her and enfolds her in his arms. He is wearing the navy cable-stitch sweater that makes him look distinguished, yet relaxed and almost young, the thick wool covering the folds of paunch below his belt.

Awkward and still blotchy from the climb, she struggles out of her boots, leaning on his shoulder, careful not to spread dirt. The parquet floor is cold to her nyloned feet. His are sheathed in backless slippers that hiss along the floor when he walks.

He calls her "*maedele,*" which means little maid, or little girl. It's a quaint term, something an aunt might say, although the way Blutstein croons the word it sounds melodic and plaintive. His first name is Mendel, but she can't call him that. It's too familiar. She's been taught to address her elders with respect, and although Blutstein has his hands up her blouse, he's still her professor and more than twice her age. Besides, Mendel is a silly name, the name someone in a comedy team might have. She calls him Blutstein in her mind and nothing to his face. Manages to complete sentences without using a name. He doesn't seem to notice.

He kisses her urgently, eyes shut tight, eyelids quivering. The great Blutstein who chose her, created her, brought her out of the awkward girlishness in which she'd been stuck, now surrenders to his creation. Now, this moment, as they hover on the brink of possibilities, is the best time of all. He shapes her into a goddess with his eyes, she reads the poetry of his face and he looks exactly as an old-world poet should: dreamy eyes under a bushy brow, sensitive lips, massive forehead, thick, wavy hair standing straight up like exclamation marks. If only they were together across a candlelit table. Or even in the living room, the beautiful living room that Rachel occasionally dares to enter, lingering over the fascinating objects that cancel out the bland rental furniture and dull winter light. Paintings of Jerusalem streets, a black-and-white photograph of a blind beggar feeling his way along an ancient wall, a copper Passover plate, a brass *menorah*, stones from the Judean desert, sun-bleached and pitted. Bits of Israel that the Blutsteins packed lovingly and brought with them to remind themselves of home. How different from her parents' house with its heathen clutter acquired during trips to Europe — the cuckoo clock, pewter beer steins, Dutch shoes, cowbells and only one cheap tin Hanukkah *menorah*, scratched from years of use, its base soiled with dusty wax.

Blutstein brings her attention back to the business at hand by nuzzling his face into her neck. His small warm hands run quickly over her body. He fumbles with her bra clasp until finally her breasts hang free and naked, although her arms are tangled in the straps. A breeze from under the front door blows against her ankles. What are they doing in the foyer? Someone passing by could hear. She pushes him toward the bedroom.

"Ah, *maedele*, you're in a hurry. Me too."

They stumble toward the guest room at the end of the hall and fall upon the single bed, Blutstein tugging at his own clothes and hers. She is glad about the existence of this little room. She couldn't bear it if they had to lie in the bed that Blutstein shares with his wife, although she wonders if he would mind so very much. The guest room doubles as study and artist's studio, with an antique wooden writing desk near the window and an empty easel on a square of paint-splotched newspaper in the opposite corner. The long wall above the desk is lined, floor to ceiling, with bookshelves on which stand massive, leather-bound tomes, their spines emblazoned with gilded Hebrew script that Rachel can't read, as well as rows of more modern texts. A few drops from the ocean of learning that Blutstein swims in daily and that she is only just beginning to glimpse.

Now Blutstein is panting, his face almost purple, clownish. An embarrassed laugh bubbles near her lips, which he interprets as desire.

"*Maedele*," he moans. He pushes himself inside her. It doesn't hurt because he's not too big. The first moment of strangeness passes quickly and the thrusts become a dull rhythm, like falling rain. The lower half of her body is quiet and far away. But they forgot the towel. She should have a towel under her to protect the bedspread, which is beautiful, a rich heavy cotton, striped red, orange, mauve, blue and purchased by Mrs. B. in the Old City of Jerusalem. Rachel dreams of such a bedspread for herself. If she isn't careful now, they will leave behind a chalky smear and a telltale smell. She will have to swing off the bed with her legs held together when he's done.

Propping himself up on his hands, he looks down on her and his face, pulled by gravity, becomes a slack mask, puffy, inflamed. A vein in his temple throbs, reminding her of his heart condition. What would she do...but she mustn't think. She doesn't want him to waste time with fondling and foreplay, although that's what the books say is supposed to happen. She becomes alarmed when he caresses her longer than usual and in places he doesn't normally touch, puts an end to his fumbling with a bold gesture of her own. She can't imagine writhing with him as she does by herself in her own bed at night. The vein in his temple, the ticking clock, the hums and stirrings of the apartment, and any moment his wife might burst through the door to find them like this. She imagines Mrs. Blutstein's frozen eyes glaring down at her over her husband's naked back. In her mind Rachel pleads, *this is not what it seems*. Then what is it? A prelude. A preparation for the more important and devastating encounter that comes after the sex.

"Are you ready?" he gasps.

She smiles. He falls upon her, finished. Excitement drains out of him, his heartbeats fade, his body presses down on her chest. She doesn't move, takes shallow breaths, testing herself. How still can she be? How long can she bear his weight? The longer he crushes down on her, the more he will be restored, refreshed, grateful. The more of a woman she will be.

"Was it good?" he says, rolling over at last.

"It was," she lies. An unimportant lie.

❧

Dressed again, the bed straightened, stray hairs and stains wiped away with a damp cloth, they prepare to sit at the writing desk near the window and drink coffee. She's less nervous now, even though danger still lies just outside the door. A step in the hall, a key in the lock and her world could come crashing down. But he has fox ears, he reassures her, and cat's feet and a sixth sense. He knows everything there is to know about escape.

He brews the coffee double strength in an enamel percolator on the stovetop. Rachel doesn't follow into the kitchen while he pours and stirs, because the pots, the potholder with the burnt thumb, all the domestic objects say *wife, wife, wife.* Instead, Rachel waits by the writing desk in the guest room, her gaze drawn to the painting on the wall: an explosion of yellow dots against an expanse of blue sea and a signature in the corner. Leah Blutstein. *Mimosa Tree at Caesarea,* it's entitled. The yellow balls wrap Rachel in sunshine, the cool blue invites her in. There is no reproach here, only kindness and wonder at yellow rapture and blue beginnings.

They hid together from the Germans. They've been married for 27 years.

Blutstein enters with a rattling tray, cups of coffee, a plate with Rachel's mother's cake. He likes this *Apfeltorte.* It is buttery and bad for the heart. He chuckles as he eats, scattering crumbs across his lap and under the desk. He pats her knee at the alarm in her eyes. Don't worry, his chuckle says. I know everything there is to know about risk. This is no risk. This is child's play.

"*Maedele,*" he says aloud, "How *are* you?" A question

that requires no answer beyond a smile. He strokes her cheek, suddenly pensive.

"One of these days you have to find a boyfriend, a nice Jewish boy. I'm keeping an eye out, but those *pishers* in my class, they're not worth much."

"Oh, no," she says, alarmed, unable to read his face. Is he serious? She can see him as matchmaker, well meaning and tactless, nudging her toward the same kind of clean-cut youth her parents would approve of, oblivious to her humiliation. She shudders, but he shrugs, hands her a steaming cup, his thoughts already elsewhere. The coffee is black and sweet, makes her jumpy if she drinks too much. On him, it has no effect except to deepen his gaze and prick his memories.

"In my hometown, at my *Rebbe's* court we drank coffee like this. No, actually, it was stronger. Twice as strong." He sits up, lips pursed in thought, eyebrows raised, listening for his story. His gaze travels far beyond the realities of this room, leaping past the walls, the bed, the cake crumbs, the painting, into a whirlwind of times and places. How magnificent his face, she thinks. It justifies everything. The lines of concentration on his forehead, the electric hair, his mouth a small, tense seed about to burst open.

"You sniffed the coffee and your mind flew up into another realm. Coffee and the Hassidic *Rebbe*," he sighs. "Much more potent than your hippie hash." He pronounces it "hesh," but she doesn't smile. She clenches the chair as she leans forward to listen, knowing that he has stories like the sky has rain and that they will soon break over her head.

"We talked of Talmud all night long. Amazing discussions. You think Talmud is dry and legalistic. No! It's alive, teeming with stories, questions, parables, great insights cutting into the core of existence. The *goyim* had an inkling of the greatness of our holy books and they were envious. This is the source of European Jew hatred. They couldn't bear that we possess a greater wisdom than their own. Ah, you don't believe me, *maedele*, but it's true."

There it is again, *goy* and Jew, clear borders marked with barbed-wire fences. What he says is too simplistic, like the words in the Bible "God hardened Pharaoh's heart," making the hatred inherent and preordained. The world is new, she wants to say. It's the Age of Aquarius. We're banding together to ban the bomb.

"There are other victims now. Vietnam."

He rakes his hair with his hands. "Can you possibly think there is any comparison? Wars are horrible, yes. But what I lived through was not a war with one side and another, one army and another. Let me tell you...."

He tells. Reveals to her what he never does in class: the dark source of his brilliance.

It begins with a picture of a ghetto. Jews from the whole region have been crowded into the quarter, sometimes 10 people forced to live in one room. Yet life goes on: work, school, markets, even concerts. But then the roundup. The rooms with their careful partitions of curtains and cots ranged along walls spew forth broken glass, bedding, copybooks, bodies and a shrieking stampede herded by men with whips and guns and before long not a soul is left in the streets, only the dogs licking the bloody stones.

She leans forward to listen with greedy interest, devouring his words but digesting none. She hears and doesn't hear as his eyes grow fierce and he shakes the air around him with both hands.

"They ransacked our town for the last of the Jews, yanked

them out of chimneys, attics, pits. Children, mothers with infants, the old and the sick driven into the marketplace. Our great *Rebbe* sat on the bare ground and recited psalms. There was blood on his lips where he'd been hit with a rifle butt. Blood dripped with every line of prayer."

She believes. She doesn't believe. She is a *Yecke*, a coward, clings to wishy-washy moderation. His stories are obscene. She lusts for more.

"...more and more people in the marketplace...no water...the blazing sun...hours and hours...the thirst...little girls offer themselves to the soldiers...mothers howl...shots into the crowd...an infant ripped from its mother's breast...and they played marching music and they set up pots to boil their pig's knuckle soup and they ate and drank while we vomited and bled, until everyone was in the cattle cars or dead, every last soul, except for me under a heap of corpses. I clawed my way up through the dead."

He claws the air, his voice chokes, the vein at his temple throbs.

Please stop, please stop. You'll keel over and I won't know what to do and she'll walk in and it will be my fault.

"I found a remnant of Jews in the forest. We bribed a peasant to let us dig a pit in his barn. We took turns keeping watch. Water-soaked straw, our clothes rotted, the lice, the worms. Quick, someone's coming...cover the entrance... stifling dark...no air...crushing our lungs...we cling to one another...her nails in my flesh, my nails in hers...hanging on for one more moment because they're here, the Germans, the peasants, the police, the partisans, to drag us out of the pit, to sell us to the Gestapo, one more Jew to kill. One more Jew to kill."

It is time for Rachel to leave. Mrs. Blutstein's class ends

at ten o'clock. She must escape out the door. Blutstein clasps her hand.

"Why did we stay alive after everyone dear to us was dead and when every moment was hell? It was a miracle, but not a pretty miracle. God bit into our hearts. Why were we spared? To bear placards for communist dictators who spit on the Jews?"

She rises to leave, but he holds her down.

"*Maedele*, stay a while, there's still time."

He has more to tell her, nicer stories. About the Holy Land that she must visit. How beautiful to walk in Jerusalem as *Shabbas* begins, the traffic stills, the dusk descends and voices flow out of the synagogues into the echoing streets, "Come let us greet her, the Sabbath bride."

A peace comes into his eyes. Now is the time to go, while he is calm and contemplative and she can slip out the door like a puff of air, leaving nothing of herself behind. But he jumps up from his chair, bends over and kisses her, a long insistent kiss, sucking her lips, then presses her face against his chest so that she can hear the irregular *ka-thunk, thunk* of his heart.

"So good with you," he moans, pulling her to her feet. "You take me out of myself. You understand? I need this."

He holds her tightly so that they are welded together, become an unbalanced mass, swaying dangerously. She is afraid they will topple onto the bed, which is perhaps what he wants, to once again...quickly...his hands begin to search.

She jerks free and bolts for her coat and boots, flung into a corner behind the guest room door. Look at the time, she pleads.

"Ah yes, the time. My little *Yecke*, so conscious of the time." He sighs, rubs his flushed face, then whacks her a smart one across the bum, which is thrust out slightly as she struggles with her boots. But she's seen it coming and holds herself steady against the wall.

"See you in class," he grins and winks, opening the front door.

She runs, runs, down 126 steps, boots echoing up the stairwell, the stale air pricking her nostrils, out into the fresh air of a winter's day where the cars still swish through the slush and the store at the corner still advertises Pepsi and Craven A. Nothing has happened in these streets of solid, blank-faced buildings, these stupid unmoved streets. A foul energy runs from the top of her head to the balls of her feet, crimping her toes. She wants to kick the metal garbage can set out neatly by the sidewalk and spill its contents into the path of oncoming pedestrians. All day, every day, images flicker beneath his eyelids, yet he grins and chuckles, eats cake and gropes for her breasts. She tries to hold onto just one image for an instant but it dissolves — *we clung together*.

She envisions the marchers, the righteous shouts, the cleverly worded placards: "Peace in the world, not the world in pieces." They lilt the words, link arms, hoot, holler, jostle, tumble together, sweep her aside. But she will burst upon them with a God-given fury, smash their signs, bash heads, kick and bite, bite, bite into their throats.

She leans against a wall outside the library, dizzy, nauseous, chilled with sweat. Buttery *torte* and coffee gurgle in her stomach. Rage has burst through her and left her empty, holding onto a wall of striated concrete. A good wall. It offers its indifferent support, asking nothing in return.

She sits in the carpeted stillness of the library, amid cool fluorescent lights and neutral colours. Outside the window, across the campus she can see the crowd gathering, from this distance a small, grey swarm with placards half-hidden behind the bare limbs of trees. They must have megaphones but she can't hear a thing, the double glazing of the window-panes muffling all sound. There's still time to join them, time to decide whether one silent, unchanting marcher would add anything to the cause.

In the meantime, she writes notes in her exercise book, soothed by the clear blue rule lines and her own round script. "Hassidism," she writes. "Popular religious movement that swept Jewish communities of eastern Europe in 18th century. Led by master-teachers, wonder-workers. Taught piety, fervour, humility, joy."

Her hand wanders across the page. *Leah*, it writes. A strong name. She must be home by now and is bustling about the kitchen preparing his lunch, listening with half an ear to his chatter. She scolds him for the crumbs strewn all over the writing desk while he grins, shamefaced and sly. But she says nothing more. She *knows*, though. Oh, yes, she must. He may be a fox, but she is a cat, knows all the games of hide-and-seek as well as he does. She lived in a pit, just as he did. She lived in a pit *with him*.

After he leaves to teach his own class, what will she do? Cry? Howl into the empty air? No, no, she won't. She will grab hold of that old anger and disappointment, bring out canvas and easel, brushes and paints, and create a cascade of blossoms against an ochre-coloured wall. *Bougainvillaea in Jerusalem*, she might call it. A brilliant purple bush, burning with a fierce inner light. Burning its presence into the room.

Edith Teilheimer's War

On October 3, 1973, during the Days of Awe, Edith Teilheimer emerged from the stuffy cocoon of an El Al plane and hesitated at the top of the metal steps that descended to Israel. Heat and light assaulted her. Joy and anxiety fluttered in her breast as she noticed the blue-and-white flags on the roof of the terminal building. She was back in the land that she'd abandoned, and that had abandoned her, almost 25 years ago, shortly after its birth.

Her doctor in England had warned her against coming.

"You've lost two stone since I saw you last," Dr. Gilmore said. He fixed her with his cool, reasonable gaze. "You're on the verge of collapse. You need rest."

But rest in the deathly quiet of a Sussex cottage was killing her. It was draining her lifeblood, burying her in moss and mildew and unsettling dreams. Since Mr. Farley had died, she'd been paralyzed by despair. She should have been glad, relieved of the drudgery of tending to an old invalid, economically secure for the first time in her life as heir to his house. But unnameable terrors lurked in the lush growth of the garden, the empty whispering rooms. She was afraid to stand still, worked late into the night housecleaning, buoyed by black coffee and pep-up pills. Her childhood aversion to food came back. She was especially disgusted by English fare, all those rich creams and fatty meats. Dr. Gilmore gave her diet supplements — a thick liquid that felt like mucus in her throat and that she poured down the drain. At night she woke from a dream of a familiar, beast-like breath in her ears.

When she saw an ad in the paper: HIGH HOLY DAYS IN ISRAEL. BARGAIN RATES, she grabbed the phone, ordered the ticket. Immediately she regretted the impulse, yet willed herself forward, remembering olive trees in the sun, her young self at a window overlooking Jerusalem, the once warm embrace of the homeland.

The surge of passengers prodded Edith down the steps and across the heat-softened tarmac. The terminal's lobby was packed. People shouted, chattered, argued, as they inched forward in the bulging line toward the customs and immigration counters. Iron railings had been set up to contain the flow, but did not. The mass of sweating bodies, luggage, children spilled around the barriers.

"You still feel the plane? Me too," said a voice nearby as Edith clutched a railing to steady herself. "The ground goes up, down, up, down." The speaker was a stocky, heavily made- up woman laden with shopping bags from Orly Airport. "*Oish*, I'm hot." She fanned herself ineffectually with her hand, an unguarded weariness in her eyes.

Back in the land where people complained loudly about their ailments to total strangers. Edith looked away, pretending not to hear.

"Are you a visitor or do you live here?" The woman, who'd been speaking Hebrew, now demanded in English.

Edith had expected busybody questions, but not so soon.

"A visitor," she said, shrinking against the railing.

"First time?" The woman peered at Edith with frank curiosity.

"Yes," Edith almost shouted, then turned away to fumble in her hand luggage.

Where would such inquiries lead? To where and how and with whom she had once lived. To Captain Peter Mackenzie, member of His Majesty's army of occupation in Palestine. During the war against Hitler it hadn't mattered that she was a Tommy's girlfriend. Jews and British were fighting the same enemy, relations were cordial, her people's struggle for liberation had been postponed. Everything changed after VE Day. The British Mandate government with its vexing ambiguities — the promise of a Jewish homeland on the one hand, the rigid immigration quotas on the other — became intolerable. The Jewish press railed against the cruel blockade of refugee ships crammed with survivors from the death camps. For a time, even more so than the Arabs, the British were the enemy. Had 25 years and other wars completely erased that fact? Edith doubted it. Jewish memory went back to Abraham.

Yet the land had grown up in her absence, had it not? Travellers from all over the world now pressed into the terminal building of Ben Gurion Airport. There were boys like hoboes with long, unkempt hair, girls in flimsy dresses and bare, black-soled feet, yet no one paid much attention, no more so than in London. Posters of Jerusalem, with joyful captions about a city reunited, smiled down from the walls. Other vistas showed date palms, vineyards, a kibbutz in the Galilee. She had never been on a kibbutz. How good it must be to give oneself over to hard, hot fieldwork, "to conquer the land with the sweat of one's brow" as the old Zionist pamphlets used to say.

She had lived in the city, although it was a strange sort of city, Jerusalem, a cluster of enclaves within the hills, a dance of towers, monuments, ancient walls, never quite real. They looked like the picture on the last page of the Passover Haggadah.

Her heart jumped. It was her turn at the immigration counter, her turn to speak to the official with hairy ears and piercing eyes.

"The purpose of your trip?" The official flipped through her passport, peered at the photo and the pathetic facts summarizing her life. Born in Germany, British subject, Jewish face. Female. Four foot ten. No distinguishing marks.

"Visiting...some places," she said, staring at the badge on his short-sleeved khaki shirt.

"You visit relatives, friends?"

"No." *Who would remember her with sympathy and who with disdain? Former lovers of former enemies not welcome.*

"Your first visit?"

The official had glanced up, his eyes narrowed.

"I lived in Jerusalem once," she blurted out. *The Jerusalem of the Mandate years when General Barker held us all under his thumb.*

"Ah, *Yerushalayim!*" The official flashed a toothy smile. His ear hairs seemed to quiver their assent. "Beautiful."

Her chest relaxed, her breath eased as he stamped her passport. *"Shanah Tova,"* he called after her as he waved her through.

"Yes," she shouted in her mind as she staggered with her luggage toward the taxi stand. "A good new year." A simple

Hebrew greeting she hadn't heard for ages. Joy and gratitude flowed through her. She was right to have come.

Dr. Gilmore would have her in a rest home. "Either that, or get your sister from Canada to come and take care of you."

She couldn't explain, neither to him nor to Hannah, that what she needed was the opposite — activity, movement, escape from the helplessness that had assailed her, escape from an England that could never be home, no matter how long she lived there.

The last six years had been good ones, relatively speaking. Working as Mr. Farley's live-in help, she'd felt settled, the restlessness and loneliness that had gnawed at her much of her life abated. He was a kind gentleman, widowed, childless like herself, appreciative of her company in front of the telly and for cards. She threw herself with satisfying fury into housework and gardening and seldom thought about the failed relationships and missed opportunities with men, or about Peter, the greatest failure of them all. But Mr. Farley's death had left her floating in a void.

Once, long ago, for a short time admittedly, she had belonged somewhere. She could walk down Ben Yehuda Street in Jerusalem and recognize Mr. Ehrlich who had known her uncle in Frankfurt, or Danny Lipshitz who'd been with her sister Hannah in the Zionist agricultural school. She could drop in on Hannah and Ernst and her little nephew and niece. She could see a knot of people on the sidewalk listening to the radio news that blared from a café and the same current of feelings — worry or anger or joy — would run through them all. She would know the rightness and wrongness, the wisdom and stupidity of all the café philosophers' arguments; they were her arguments, too. This web held her close. She was not yet outside the linked arms of the circle.

❧

Edith pressed herself against the window and away from the crush of other passengers in the shared cab. The *sheroot* lurched and sped down the narrow highway toward Tel Aviv, past orange groves, irrigated fields, factories and sprawling settlements that she remembered as a cluster of tin shacks. Smells of fertilizer, pesticide, concrete dust were woven through with the smell of the majestic eucalyptus trees planted in long rows by the side of the road. The October sun blazed with the accumulated force of a long, hot summer and glinted off an approaching forest of television antennas. Yes, the country had grown and prospered. No longer a mere sliver pressed against the sea, it now encompassed all of Sinai, the Golan, the West Bank. How much had Jerusalem changed? Would the building she once lived in on King George Street still exist?

She wasn't sure what she wanted to find there beyond a glimpse of her younger self, the girl who had stood at that window full of stupid, beautiful hope. When her father had died she was at last free of his religious tyranny, no longer forced to live in his dingy apartment in Tel Aviv. She had rented her own room in Jerusalem, paid for with her own money, kitchen and bathroom privileges included and shared with only Mrs. Yanofsky and her young nephew, Shmulik. Though the room was small and poorly furnished, the view overlooking the city more than made up for the sagging mattress and the cans of petrol strategically positioned to keep bedbugs away. From her window she could see rooftops descending toward Jaffa Road, the YMCA tower, the King David Hotel and in the distance, ancient walls, the Mount of Olives, farther still, a hint of the Judean wilderness where jackals howled and Bedouin roamed.

She had a clerical job at the Labour Department and she had a man — Peter Mackenzie — movie-star handsome with his sandy hair, trim moustache, military bearing and keen, blue eyes. They had met at a gramophone concert at the Y. She'd come in late, had no program and stole glances at his, which caused him to smile and slide into the empty chair beside her. He whispered commentaries about the classical recordings into her ear as if they were old friends, so that she forgot her usual shyness. Normally, she would not have given much thought to a man like him. He was of another world — card games in the barracks, whisky in the officers' club, salmon fishing in Scotland. His foreignness and the unlikelihood of the affair leading to anything serious made her feel foreign too, as if she'd slipped into the body of a bold, flirtatious, easygoing woman. But then, his tenderness caught her off guard. "You're such a wee sprite," he would say with reverence, encircling her waist with his hands. Once she allowed herself to believe he truly cared, she became addicted to his love.

Edith opened her eyes when the cab panted to a halt at a traffic-choked intersection.

"Allenby Street," the *sheroot* driver informed those passengers in the back who might be newcomers. "Here you can get everything."

She looked out on blocks of concrete buildings, yellowed, pockmarked, some crumbling at corners and windowsills, festooned with drooping laundry, rusted railings and water tanks. At street level stood an unbroken row of shops, some small and dark, some with a jumble of goods in the doorway, others larger, with shiny new signs. The huge cavity of a construction site yawned at one corner where jackhammers pounded and cranes clattered. Buses belched fumes, vehicles with four, three and two wheels crammed the road. Men with briefcases, women with string shopping bags, rushed about. Young people strode by in jostling clusters. She gazed out the window, feeling small, lost and panic-stricken at the hectic pace, the brash, unfamiliar throngs.

Hotel Gesher was a three-star establishment near the sea, but located well behind the Sheraton and the Dan, beachfront giants that would catch the first fresh breezes of the morning, hoarding them for their well-heeled guests. Leaning over her balcony railing, though, Edith could glimpse a cheery strip of blue between the buildings. She felt light and airy inside, better than she would have thought, despite her restless night and raging thirst. Street sounds — the snarl of Vespas, shouts, laughter, the clink of glasses from the balcony next door — had kept her company through much of the night and the roar of traffic began early, so that she had a good excuse to slide out of bed when the first rays of daylight crept through the slats in the blinds. In Mr. Farley's cottage, the night had been so still she had been aware of her own irregular heartbeat and anguished sighs.

"Good morning, misery," she said aloud to her reflection in the bathroom mirror and stuck out a white-coated tongue. "You're a sight to scare the children."

She was indeed thin, pinched, her eyes bruised-looking,

the skin under her throat loose. In recent months the flesh had melted off her, but Dr. Gilmore was obsessed with the notions of an ideal weight. The numbers when she stood on the scale had to match up to figures on a chart. Why? Couldn't her body find its own equilibrium?

She dressed carefully in her beige pantsuit, coral necklace, dark glasses and straw hat and descended the three flights of stairs to the Gesher's lobby. From an adjoining room where a breakfast buffet was being served came the clink of cutlery and glasses. And what a beautiful spread it was: oranges and melons, hard-boiled eggs, marinated herring, chopped cucumber and tomato salad, paper-thin slices of cheese. The counter was decorated with vases of gladioli. She could admire the sight although she couldn't contemplate downing the quantities of food that other guests were heaping upon their plates. She poured herself a glass of ice water and took a roll, a bit of melon, a dab of cottage cheese — all that she could stomach at the moment.

"What is it, lady, you're on a diet?" said a dark-skinned youth holding a coffeepot. Smiling, winking, he indicated the buffet with a sweep of his hand. He had a bush of kinky black hair and pitted skin, but he wasn't bad-looking. His short-sleeved white shirt was open at the throat. A gold chain gleamed amid thick chest hair. His name tag said: CHAIM.

"You won't get better at the Sheraton," he said, pouring coffee into her cup, arm held high and gracefully, not spilling a drop.

"I don't usually eat breakfast."

"Of course not. You are American. No!" He slapped his forehead. "You are *Yecke*, German Jew, I know the accent. But you live in America where they eat...what? Bits of eggshell and milk for breakfast. You come to Israel, you must eat like

Israeli." He held his hand to his breast and grinned until she could not help grinning back.

"Perhaps by tomorrow morning I'll be up to it."

"Today you rest, yes? You go to the beach, lie in the sun, get some colour in that pale *Yecke* face."

"Actually I was going to Jerusalem today. What's the best way to get there?"

"No time for the beach? Just like *Yecke*, rush, rush." Chaim clicked his tongue. "The best way is by *sheroot*, of course. You walk up this street, turn right, then straight, straight, straight past Bank Ha'poalim and you will see the *sheroot*." He smiled broadly, revealing a gap in his back teeth. He shook a finger at her and swung away with an energetic stride.

A *Sfardi*, Oriental Jew. Cocky and confident and no doubt earning a good living as a waiter. In her day, the young people were mostly from Europe and German was practically the second language on the street. A whole new generation had grown up in her absence, glowing and healthy, speaking a rapid Hebrew she could barely follow, many of them wearing the same crazy fashions she'd seen on Carnaby Street. For a boy like Chaim, the Mandate era would be as unreal as ancient Egypt, and Britain would mean the Beatles and the Rolling Stones.

She set out for the *sheroot* stand to check about booking a seat and found herself on Dizengoff Street, jewel of Tel Aviv with its boutiques and cafés, though hardly the Paris some people claimed it to be. She remembered Dizengoff still unfinished, its trees tiny, stretches of sand between the newly built sidewalks. Now there were stores, banks, office buildings, crowds, a bus full of schoolchildren waving and screaming, a bevy of girls in miniskirts, soldiers of both sexes, trim and bronzed, strolling by.

They were beautiful, unbearably beautiful. Their unquenchable youth glowed against the worn concrete of buildings thrown up in haste. She had no place here. What could she offer as a middle-aged woman with spidery limbs, hollow cheeks, expired womb? She drifted on, jostled by the crowd, stumbling on the uneven sidewalk and catching sight every now and then of her reflection — an apparition in a sunhat — in plate glass windows. After some blocks she wondered if she had taken a wrong turn. The sun pressed down on her head, the air was thick, humid, stale. Was it always so hot in October or were they in the midst of a *chamsin*, the oppressive heat wave that could envelop the land several times a year? *Chamsin* in Jerusalem, she remembered, had made Peter listless, sapped of strength and desire, while having the opposite effect on her. It had quickened her blood, made her alert and energetic. She would bathe his face with wet cloths, bring him tea to cool him down as he lay limp, his long body covering almost every inch of her narrow bed.

Dizzy with heat, legs heavy, she now staggered to a table at a sidewalk café. She had walked less than 10 blocks. Washed up.

"*Tay cham,*" she said to the freckle-faced youth who came by, finally, to slap a rag around the crumbs strewn over her table. Hot tea was what she needed, strong, hot tea. Without a word or nod of response, the youth swung away and began to work over another table, an empty one. "Did you hear me?" she croaked, her throat so dry. "Of course," said the boy, addressing himself to the rag in his hand. "Take it easy,

Giveret." He sauntered off and returned a few moments later with a glass of pale, lukewarm liquid and a slice of lemon on a plate.

Shmulik, Mrs. Yanofsky's nephew, also had that manner of pretending not to hear. Shmulik, whose room had been next door to hers in that King George Street apartment.

"Where's your aunt?" Edith had asked as he slouched at the kitchen table, cracking sunflower seeds between his large, uneven teeth. His breath came out in long sighs between bites. "Will Mrs. Yanofsky be back soon?" He spat shells into his palm and did not look up.

"Shmulik, you're dreaming again," she said, trying to humour him.

He glanced sideways, finally. "She's gone to market. You can leave the rent in the jar." He spoke in gruff, Sabra staccato, but his voice cracked on the final word and his face flamed. He was an overgrown cactus of a boy with long, ungainly limbs and, eternally congested, he had a laboured way of breathing, especially while eating. Her female presence clearly disturbed him, though she was small and flat-chested, a far cry from the buxom girls he must have seen every day at school. They avoided one another as much as they could, waiting for the *click* of the neighbouring bedroom door before venturing down the hall to the toilet. Still, Edith sometimes had a prickling sensation at the back of her neck. Was he watching her?

Shmulik's parents had not made it to Palestine and perhaps never would. They were among the many refugees pounced upon by the British and sent to languish in an internment camp in Cyprus. Sometimes at night he kicked the walls of his room. He worshipped the Revisionists, agreed with their terrorist actions against the British and Arabs, muttered slogans from their pamphlets — FREEDOM OR DEATH. Over his bed hung a poster with the Revisionist symbol, a raised fist clutching a rifle over a map of Palestine and the Transjordan and the words, "Only thus." The restrained tactics of the Jewish Agency, the voice of the official Jewish community, made him laugh.

She feared for Peter; there had been kidnappings, stabbings in British barracks. But Peter assured her that Mr. Begin, though an extremist, was far too canny to enlist clumsy crackpots like Shmulik.

The *sheroot* stand was mobbed. A noisy crowd milled about on the sidewalk, but no cabs, no drivers, no one in authority seemed to be in sight. There were young Americans with knapsacks, off-duty soldiers, weary-looking mothers with squirming children and a separate knot of *yeshiva* youth in long black coats and black hats. A car suddenly sped around the corner and screeched to a halt, its doors flew open, the crowd surged forward and, amid shouts and cries, passengers squeezed into their seats, the driver flung baggage onto the roof rack.

"*Yerushalayim?*" Edith asked one of the mothers and pointed to the swarmed cab.

"No, Haifa," said the woman, wiping her sweaty face with her arm.

"Do you know where I'd find the stand for Jerusalem?" Edith craned her neck to see over the crowd that now encircled her.

"Here, right here," said the woman. "Don't worry. The next one will be for Jerusalem."

"Do you have to book a seat?"

The woman stared, incredulous. Edith began to edge away from bodies pressed around her. She smelled rank sweat and fruity perfumes, felt the jab of elbows. The woman grabbed her sleeve.

"I'm telling you, it's here for Jerusalem." Edith's stomach lurched, hot acid burned her throat, she fought through the mass that threatened to knock her down, trample her under relentless feet. Breathless, heart pounding, she hurried back toward the hotel. In the lobby, she encountered Chaim lounging with a cigarette.

"Of course the *sheroot* is busy," he said. "Tomorrow is the eve of both *Yom Kippur* and *Shabbat*." He slapped his cheek. "Double the trouble. But why go to Jerusalem? It's so religious, quiet as a grave on a holiday. In Tel Aviv, you at least have the beach."

She lay restless in her hotel bed listening to night sounds that were no longer comforting — voices, footsteps, traffic, the *click* of the ceiling fan. From somewhere came a woman's mournful call, "Michal, Mee...chal," and a cat howled in anguish into the darkness. All these noises were connected to one another, belonged to the real world that was far away, on the other side of a glass barrier, while she was adrift in empty space. She craved but resisted sleep, afraid of the crush of dreams....

"My plucky girl," said Peter, smiling down on her from a great height. "Chin up, it will soon be over." He handed her something. "Here you are, you've been looking for this." It was a razor blade encrusted with rust. She danced it across

her arm. It would be so easy, like cutting into soft cheese, but her hand shook, the blade stung but refused to sink down. One needed calm to kill oneself. "Cheerio, then," said Peter, slipping out the window. British patrol Jeeps raced by on the street below. Feet approached, an angry mob. They burst through the door of Mrs. Yanofsky's apartment, crowded into her room, panting, jostling around her bed, an elbow in her back. "Only thus," yelled Shmulik, triumphant.

She awoke to a dark room and the *click, click, click* of the ceiling fan.

"Motek, eat," said Chaim the next morning. "It's not yet *Yom Kippur*. Look at all this food." He gestured toward the hotel's breakfast buffet, which was even more lavish than the day before. A watermelon boat with a tower of melon balls — pink, yellow, green — stood as the centrepiece. Platters of smoked fish with capers and dill, marinated salads, gleaming olives, pastries, blintzes oozing cream. A line of hotel guests heaped their plates. Forks clinked, glasses tinkled.

"It's part of the price. Take as much as you want." He shook his head at her, lifted a palm in a gesture of supplication. He called her "*motek*," sweetie, as if she were an old friend, or a child.

"I've had breakfast already," Edith said, looking up at his sunny face.

"No, you have not. I watched you," he scolded.

"What are you? My mother?"

"Yes," he said, delighted. "I am Persian. No one takes care of you like a Persian. You have been sick. You have come to rest and to get strong again. How do I know? I know. I have a nose for people." He laid a forefinger on the side of his nose. "But to get strong, you must eat."

"Thank you," she said, straightening up in her chair, too weary to argue or to banter. "I'll take some more when I'm ready."

"Do it!" he said and hopped off to pour coffee for other tables. But a moment later he glanced back over his shoulder, gestured a hand spooning food to his mouth, shook his finger at her so that she had to laugh. A sweet boy. A child. She would have liked a child like him. How could she explain the treachery of food? Postcard-perfect on the buffet table, it became cold pudding in your gut, sloshed around all morning and left a foul aftertaste in your mouth.

She went to the beach, thinking the sea air would refresh her and clear away the almost drunken sensation she'd had ever since she'd left the plane. She rented a deck chair with an awning, a tiny enclave of shade under the fierce glare of the sun. Eons ago, before Hannah was married, the two of them had come down to Tel Aviv together and spent an afternoon by the sea, the only outing she remembered ever taking with her sister in all those years. They had no money so they sat in the sand, in the shade of the backs of other people's deck chairs. They peeked between the armrests at the young men passing by, giggled like schoolgirls and sang old favourites. "*Ich bin von Kopf bis Fuss...*" they drawled, imitating Dietrich. One tiny grain of time, sparkling and perfect, the only one she can remember.

She had never been completely happy with Peter. He blew hot and cold, one minute tender, almost slavish with his great head in her lap, his blue eyes gazing up at her. But then, if she allowed herself to look at him with too much need in her eyes, he pulled away, with a polite smile and light banter, as if she were a stranger, someone to pass the time with on a train station platform.

He was reluctant to introduce her to any of his army mates, for her own sake, he said. They were all right really, good enough chaps in their way, but they could let slip a remark or two, not unkindly meant, just a way of talking. "And you wouldn't let it pass. You'd be pressing them for their views about Abraham, Isaac and Jacob on down."

Her own people disapproved of him too, some quite openly, others through their pointed silence, although Peter had been welcome at her sister's and brother-in-law's home. Ernst and Peter would sit on stools under the awning that protruded over the entrance to the rooftop apartment and talked about the viability of the proposed Jewish state, taking on roles contrary to what one might expect.

"Trust in your captain, Ben Gurion," said Peter, slapping Ernst on his bony knee.

"He means well," said Ernst afterward, stripping to his undershirt with visible relief, now that company was gone. "But one can have an overly romantic view of things from the safety of the Allenby barracks." Hannah looked at Edith with anxious eyes, reading the latest disappointment in her sister's face.

"What would your father say, blessed be his memory?" said Edith, imitating the shocked voice and singsong accent of Mr. Ehrlich from Frankfurt. Her father, had he lived to see her with Peter, would have sat *shiva*. She would have become orphaned more entirely than through his physical death. This thought was both terrible and satisfying because it confirmed what she already knew, that the daughter he had laid claim to was an idea, a notch on the family tree, and all those weekly Sabbath blessings, his strong hands upon her head, had been empty gestures.

She dozed in the deck chair, woke and squirmed with the discomfort of a stiffening spine. It was not good for her back, this arc of cloth that held her uncomfortably suspended, but she was too tired and dispirited to move just yet. The sea winked and flashed. Young women in skimpy bikinis passed by. Young men wheeled around and trotted after them. Children dashed toward the waves. A pair of lovers kissed with carefree abandon, clinging together, eyes shut tight, while the crowd flowed around them unperturbed. In Jerusalem, in the old days, you were never anonymous. You smiled longingly at a man with the wrong shape of nose and Mr. Ehrlich who'd known your uncle in Frankfurt, took note, wondered aloud what your father would say.

As the months had passed it had become harder to appear with Peter in public. The streets grew tense and fearful. A massive explosion ripped apart the King David Hotel. The British conducted roundups and house-to-house searches. Begin promised to drive out the British by "blood and fire." The Jewish Agency denounced both his "gang of desperadoes" and the British retaliations. More bombings, kidnappings, executions, endless deliberations in London and New York about the partition of Palestine, British soldiers killed in their sleep, Jewish civilians shot by drunken British soldiers, curfews, martial law and, finally, the division of the city into enclaves, all government buildings and British residential quarters cordoned off, barricaded behind thickets of barbed wire.

She received a note in the mail with Jeremiac denunciations, written in a large, childish scrawl; "The wild ass in the wilderness lifts her rump for any stranger! Vile harlot! Polluter of the land!" The note was folded around a clipping from a local Hebrew newspaper — a cartoon of a pig in a British officer's uniform.

"Better that we separate until things settle down," Peter said, lifting her chin gently. "Cheer up, old girl. Worst comes to worst, your people will throw us out and you'll have your state." But was it concern for her welfare that made him stay away? Or had he sought an excuse? She heard rumours about a girlfriend from the French consulate. She wandered Jerusalem, drawn to the barricades, peering across fences at clusters of soldiers, meeting the hard stares of an army under siege. Had he been hurt in the "troubles"? Had he been taken to hospital? The authorities dithered about divulging information. She thought she glimpsed him in the glare at a street corner and behind the glass of a tobacconist's shop. She searched for weeks, feeling his presence around every bend, unaware that he'd already left the country, been shipped back home for an extended leave. Unaware, too, that he was struck with nostalgia from the moment he saw the port of Haifa disappearing and the mountains of the Carmel sink toward the sea. From the distance of England, he missed his plucky girl. She was small, bright, tender-lipped, he had written later, like the bright flowers that pushed between the stones of Jerusalem's walls.

ભ

You close your eyes and you become a relic in a deck chair, your youth flies away after a scuffle with the night.

She needed action, the soothing rhythm of physical work, to pour what was left of her broken life into the land. On a street near her hotel she found the jam-packed, hubbub-filled offices of the national kibbutz movement. The small waiting room was crowded with young people, Americans mostly, dishevelled, cheerful and chattering. They bent their heads together over brochures, they called to one another across the room, they filled out forms on their knees or braced against knapsacks. She picked her way through the crowd, stepping over the outstretched legs of girls and boys who had parked themselves on the floor, until she reached a queue in front of a lone clerk at a counter. The clerk, a woman with glasses and a pinched, irritated look, spoke to the youths leaning over the counter while a phone behind her rang incessantly. Every so often she picked it up, jabbered a bit, hung up and turned back to the supplicants in the line. The wait seemed endless. Edith swayed from foot to foot, the room heaved up and down. She tried to focus on the posters of orchards and vineyards. Work was the answer. Hot, tedious work in the fields, redeeming the land with the sweat of one's brow.

"I can give you the form," barked the clerk. She was already peering over Edith's head at the next person in line. "But your son or daughter has to come here for themselves."

"It's for me. I want to go to a kibbutz."

"For guest houses, it's somewhere else, another office."

"I want to work," Edith said in Hebrew.

The woman stared for a moment, shrugged, scribbled

something in the margin of a form and thrust it at her. "You will have to pass a physical exam. The address of the doctor is there. Who is next?"

Yom Kippur morning brought her a peace of sorts. No buffet to waylay her, no Chaim to berate her. The side room with the breakfast tables lay in darkness, the lobby sat empty except for the hotel clerk, asleep at the desk. Still, a wave of nausea assaulted her, the effects of another restless night. Ducking into the Ladies', also in darkness for some reason, she groped toward a stall and heaved liquid. Relieved, though dizzy, she splashed water onto her face, rinsed her mouth and spat. The mirror above the sink revealed a shadow, a smudge of human form that moved as she moved. She bolted into the lobby and staggered past the desk. Dragging open the front door, she stepped into the day's glare.

The city lay quiet, its stores shut tight, the usual bustle stilled. Even the radios that normally blared from every bus, cab and corner stall were silenced, all Israeli broadcasts cancelled for the High Holiday. A line of cars stood along the curb with barely a hair's breadth between them, like a train immobilized. Everyone was at prayer or asleep or at the beach. She took a long swig from the bottle of water she now carried in her purse and walked unsteadily toward Yarkon Street and the beckoning blue strip of the Mediterranean. She reached the wall that separated Yarkon from the sands and looked down. Not quite the holiday crowd you'd find on a Saturday, but scores of people, nevertheless, at the usual pursuits of swimming, sunbathing, playing paddleball. The deck chair vendor was closed, so she sank into the sand by the shade of a wall. What to do with this long, empty day? What to do with the eternity of years? How to fill even another week of her stay here? She lay dizzy in the sand, her hat over her eyes, and heard the snore of the sea and Shmulik's rasping breath in her ear, his mucusy, stuffed-up sigh.

She'd always suspected that Shmulik was one of the boys who had beaten her. She'd been wandering the streets during the "days of disorder" as the British Mandate was ending and the Jewish-Arab war began in earnest, with sniping and explosions throughout the city. She skirted the edge of neighbourhoods no longer safe, followed a convoy of soldiers, searching for *her* soldier and half expecting a knife in the back, a stone to come flying at the side of her head. She wheeled around and saw an Arab boy on a donkey, his wine-dark eyes pouring pure hatred across the lane that separated them. She hurried on. She saw no faces, only scuffling feet, as arms grabbed her and a sack of rough cloth fell over her head.

"Whore of Babylon," they'd yelled in her ear. "Traitor!" Hoarse, adolescent voices, speaking Hebrew.

She could not tell how far they dragged her. Stone walls, then steps, scraped her legs. She lay blind on a concrete floor, choked on coarse cloth as an army of feet kicked. Her body, gone numb, absorbed their blows, allowed itself to be flung, became as limp and silent and useless as dead matter. How many were there really? Perhaps only three. Shmulik's voice was not among them. But the final blow, the foot that thudded into her back, came with a familiar grunt, an ugly sound of sucked-in breath.

Afterward...but there was no afterward, no continuation of the story, no one to accuse and no one to listen to accusations. Her ribs healed, her bruises faded, she carried on, preoccupied like everyone else with the growing chaos as the British evacuated, the Arab armies struck, the siege of Jerusalem intensified. Even Hannah, who'd cried at the sight of her, then nursed her tenderly, and Ernst who'd been white with rage, could do nothing. The day-to-day struggle to endure hunger and thirst, hold together, maintain morale took over for everyone. The only story was survival. And then, the miraculous victory, the rebirth of the nation, salvation and statehood after 2,000 years of exile and pogrom. *Hatikvah* rang out through the Jewish half of the city: "As long as in the heart, the Jewish spirit yearns...the hope of 2,000 years is not lost...." Circles within circles of *hora* dancers swarmed Zion Square. "We have a state," they cried. "*Am Yisrael chai!*" The lines of dancers wove around her, grabbed hold of her and she swung too, like a puppet, back and forth and up and down. Hearts flowed together into a great, warm sea but her own heart remained ice. Shouts of joy and song joined over her head and in her ear roared the rough beast breath.

She accepted the haven in England that Peter eventually offered, but was not surprised, or even deeply disappointed, when the relationship broke apart. She had lost her taste for love.

A loud wail spiralled out of the depths of the city, blanketed the rooftops with its animal howl. The beachgoers froze. Mouths gaped. Heads tilted backward to scan the sky. The wail rose and fell, stretched on, drained blood from the heart, then died.

"Surely a false alarm," someone said.

Someone else hauled a portable radio from a knapsack, but it produced only static. "The Voice of Israel" was still off the air, as was normal for the Day of Atonement. It was just a false alarm, the cluster of people near Edith agreed, but they stirred uneasily, and the man with the radio continued to twiddle the dials. Then suddenly, an announcer spoke: "When the siren sounds again, everyone must go to their shelters."

Mothers hauled their children out of the sand. The sunbathers grabbed their towels. Cars began to race down Yarkon Street. Edith joined the exodus from the beach into the city, a mostly quiet, briskly walking crowd.

"God's punishment," cried a man draped in a *tallit*, pointing at the bare legs and sandalled feet, the un-holy-day garb, passing by. But no one paid attention. Their silence seemed to say his ranting was too frivolous, the business at hand too serious to bother with God-talk now.

At the hotel, the lobby buzzed, a group of bewildered guests and staff huddled around the radio set up on the front desk, waiting for another announcement. In the meantime, there was music: Beethoven's *Moonlight Sonata*. After several hours, the news finally came. "The Egyptians have crossed the Suez...fierce fighting in Sinai...full mobilization...private cars to be requisitioned...all non-emergency patients in hospitals to return home...."

Edith listened carefully, although she found some of the Hebrew too hard to follow. Her limbs shook, her heart pounded. The sound of the siren had entered her body, as had the alarm of the hotel guests, the anxiety of the people pouring out of the synagogues, the concern in the radio announcer's voice.

She returned upstairs thinking to rest and calm her nerves, but could not stay still, paced the narrow lanes between the bed and the dresser and from bathroom to balcony. Through the walls she could hear commotion in other rooms, the ringing of phones, the clamour of voices.

"The airlines are putting on extra flights," said a man who was dusting out a suitcase on the neighbouring balcony.

She drifted toward the lobby and encountered Chaim at the bottom of the stairs. A different Chaim. For a moment she didn't know who he was. He wore the olive-green uniform of a soldier, tidy and trim, the pant legs tucked into high-topped boots. A green beret was stretched over his head, hiding his hair and making his nose look bigger, more serious. An Uzi hung from his shoulder and his fingers tapped along the barrel nervously.

"Oh, Chaim!" she heard herself call out. The sight of him stabbed her heart. The terrible efficiency of the uniform. The gold chain around his neck was gone, replaced by a metal one at the end of which, she knew, was a tag with his name and serial number — that scrap of identification which might be found should his body be blown apart.

"Madam, you must go back home. Call your airline. Or just get a taxi to the airport. They will have extra flights." Gone was his flirtatious charm. His manner was brusque and businesslike, almost harsh.

"I don't want to leave," she said.

"But you must. I've been mobilized. The hotel may close down, who knows. This is no time for tourists."

"I'll work. I'll volunteer on a kibbutz."

Chaim sucked his teeth with impatience. "You're a sick woman. Go home. You'll only be a burden." He pushed her gently toward the stairs, then turned and hurried out the front door.

"Take care," she called toward his retreating back.

She stood still some time longer, then knew what to do. She walked in the same direction as Chaim, through the front door and into the now bustling street. Dusk had fallen. Neon signs and traffic lamps flashed. She needed to find a store where she could buy a few provisions in case, indeed, the state of emergency was prolonged. Just some essentials — nuts, fruit, bread, cheese, bottled water. The food would last her a long time, longer than it would the toughest soldier, she would have liked to tell Chaim. During the siege of Jerusalem, she'd shared her ration of bread with Hannah's children and learned to make soup out of weeds. If she couldn't fight or work now, no matter. She could watch and wait and sorrow and exchange words with the street-corner philosophers and meet the eyes of grief-struck mothers. Her legs felt strong beneath her. She was calm and ready for the battle ahead.

Maladies of the Inner Ear

*I*n the Hauptmarktplatz outside Gerda's window all is confusion — the whine of engines, slam of metal doors, footsteps, shouts, murmurs, entreaties, cries. She presses her face into the pillow, but the din continues. Now the noises order themselves into a steady rhythm, a thick *tramp, tramp, tramp* of a thousand boots on flagstones; they approach, recede, approach, recede. Sickening as this is, what follows is worse. For now all is still except for the splash of water from the fountain in the middle of the square. It is a tall, spire-shaped masterpiece of intricate stonework, this fountain — the town's showpiece with its tier upon tier of stone figures from the 12th century. Cascades of water run down the faces and robes of saints, prophets, popes and noblemen, bathe their stone eyes. Inches from her ear, it seems, water pummels the ground with merciless *smacks*. She tosses her head sideways. No escape.

In the bedroom of her luxury apartment in Toronto's Forest Hill, Dr. Gerda Levittson is finally fully awake and staring at a familiar trapezoid of reflected light on the ceiling. The cacophony of the Hauptmarktplatz is over, replaced by a shapeless, nameless roaring. Something like a sea is in her head. It thrashes against the walls of her skull with dizzying, deafening force. It is what Gerda calls her demon and she senses its laughter as she drowns and drowns in noise, is sucked under by foul despair.

With effort, she pushes herself into sitting position. She fumbles in the drawer for her hearing aid and pushes the cool moulded plastic into her ear. As she raps with her knuckles, testing, on the bedside table, this blessed sound from the outer world penetrates. *Tap, tap.* A message of hope, calm and real. She switches on the radio. Late-night jazz. Muffled trumpet notes above the waves.

Outside, the night is black beyond the glow of the streetlamp. It is 2:16 a.m. The sleeping pills that were supposed to deliver her into morning haven't worked. Time, perhaps, to administer a higher dosage. Insomnia is the worst part of the affliction that has tormented her for the past two months. Same for everyone. This fact is confirmed not only by the medical journals and textbooks, but by the sighs and moans of fellow group members. Those like herself, who are new to the misery, have the pale, strained faces and nervous tics of insomniacs.

Each one hears something different. Mr. Somerville, self-appointed chairperson of the group, hears the distant but persistent drone of an airplane. Lucy hears crickets and sometimes, on a very bad day, the sound of smashing china. Bob hears the crackle of radio static, as if his head were caught between channels. "I keep wanting to adjust the dial," he says with a wry grin, while his fingers twitch.

Gerda switches on the bedside table lamp and attempts to read more of her novel, but the words swim on the page and the clamour worsens. Learn to live with it, they say in her group. Learn to relax and accept the rushing, roaring wind in the cave as if it were as normal and natural as the ticking of a clock. So it abates, becomes background noise and you can hear yourself think. Interesting phrase. Never, until now, has she realized what it meant, or what its *opposite* might mean. The steady inner voice that has kept her company for 75 years is now gone, roughly expelled. She won't find it again until the dawn spreads its calm, grey light through her apartment and solid edges reappear — top of the dresser, silver frame around the family portrait circa 1932 — father, mother, Ludwig and herself, a plump, bespectacled adolescent.

Friday nights back in Germany. The dinner table laden with gilt-edged serving dishes that offered up smells of roast chicken, dumplings, challah and wine. The family kept the commandments, but in moderation, according to their liberal faith, and in the time-honoured, decorum-loving way of the German Jewish bourgeoisie. On Saturday, although Gerda's father closed the store, he went in to do accounts in the shuttered gloom or to sort through order forms and samples of material — tweeds from England, silks from Japan. On Friday evening, they all gathered around the dining room table, lit candles, murmured blessings in Hebrew and German and tucked into the courses that the maid put before them. Her father with his stern bulldog face sat distracted, stealing glances at the neatly folded newspaper at his elbow. Her mother, thin and wan in the light of the Sabbath candles, was already showing the signs of illness. The family was able to see her safely to her grave shortly after the first volley of boycotts and decrees and before the Law for the Protection of German Blood and German Honour.

Her brother, Ludwig, was 26, a teacher at the leading progressive, secular school. He was remote and handsome with a neat moustache and wavy hair trained back to show off his high, noble forehead. With his confident laugh, he teased her about her lessons, what she didn't remember or hadn't yet learned. He recited Heine: "'Oh Germany, distant love of mine...' Well, what comes next?" Her cheeks flushed with indignation. She could have told him about the stages of photosynthesis, but he asked the wrong questions.

Her father mumbled his abbreviated version of *Birkat Hamazon*, "Grace after Meals." "Lord our God...sustains the whole world...food to all creatures...may the Merciful One reign...."

Before the amen, and despite entreaties from their mother, Ludwig was up from his chair and dashing toward the hall.

"What a way to behave. You'll spoil your digestion."

He sat his fedora on his head, blew a kiss and was gone. They knew he was off to the Hauptmarktplatz where young people gathered on Friday and Saturday nights to exchange news and argue politics. But mostly they went to flirt and to court or be courted. Arm in arm, newly matched couples paraded around the perimeter of the square, while those still single clustered in small groups by the fountain. Ludwig was in great demand.

It is dark. It is the middle of the night. Outside, beyond Forest Hill's stately homes, the woods of the ravine lie still in the heavy air. The sweet, rotting smell of late August wafts through the window. She would like to walk outside right now, in her nightgown, into the embrace of the bathwater-warm air but...muggers and maniacs. This too is new, this timidity. A few months ago, Dr. Gerda Levittson, despite her age, her deafness, her cane, walked the most secluded paths of the park whenever she pleased. Former patients, whose faces she always remembered although she forgot their names, greeted her with delight. "It's just not the same since you retired," an old-timer would say. "The young ones these days don't know how to listen."

She went once a month to Rinaldo's Hair Design to have her favourite colour, Sunset Glow, reapplied by Rinaldo's deft hands. Afterward, as she stumped along through the crowds in Yorkville, she chuckled to herself at a passerby's occasional startled glance or indulgent smile. This wonderful parade of fashionable young people in their leathers and silks and studied indifference.

But her heart is no longer in Rinaldo's and Yorkville. The hairdryer bothers her, the smells and most of all being confined in the chair with the hot, sticky plastic apron tied tight around her neck. She wonders whether, beneath the cooing encouragement, Rinaldo has been laughing at her all these years. Her real colour, yellowish grey, has grown back in, pushing the band of orange-red away from her head and looking, for the first few weeks, like a gaudy, badly arranged bandanna.

She reaches under the bed for her notepad and pen to work on the little talk on medications she is preparing for her group.

"*Tinnitus*," she has written. "From the Latin, meaning to toll or ring like a bell. It can be almost any kind of noise

— a hissing, whistling, crackling, grinding, roaring, thrumming, clicking, chirping, pulsing, rattling, booming (or any combination of these) or even a tune, endlessly, distractingly repeated. It is a symptom, not a disease. Some possible causes: an increase of fluid in the inner ear, pressure on nerve fibres due to infections, tumours, multiple sclerosis, muscular spasms, circulation problems, reactions to drugs, caffeine, alcohol, loud noises, hormonal changes, anxiety, depression, shock."

Two-thirty a.m. The endless night creeps on its belly.

She reaches for the telephone, longs to hear her name spoken by a friend, words to anchor her, but who at this hour...? Although Hannah Birnbaum in Montreal might be willing to talk, it would be Ernst who would answer the phone, dazed, worried, then somewhat annoyed by her assurances that everything was all right, that she just wanted to chat. And Hannah would be distressed beyond all proportion because her Gerda had always been the strong one. Months ago, Hannah had phoned, depressed and lonely. Gerda, setting out for her afternoon ramble, had suggested joining a group, though she knew full well Hannah was incapable of reaching out to strangers. Later she called back and apologized for her curtness and they reminisced about old times, the youth group in Germany — the outings, flirtations, misadventures.

"Remember," Hannah said, "the day I knocked over the bench during the talk on kibbutz life? I almost howled with laughter!"

Hannah had been lovely then, innocent and bumbling as a calf, driven by a restless yearning for nature. On outings in the country she trembled with rapture at the sight of a tumbled-down wall overgrown with wildflowers, while Gerda collected botanical specimens.

Before Hitler, and for many months afterward, the youth group had been about camaraderie, purpose and fun, an escape from cold shoulders and outbreaks of violence on the streets. Serious business, yes, but only to a point. Anyway, who took the Zionist rhetoric literally? Not even the leaders who wrote the manifestos. Ludwig, of course, had always scoffed at the "little ghetto in Palestine" and at propaganda that stressed divisions between Germans and Jews. One learned to shut out ugliness, to make much of small triumphs, to bear insults — a complaint about the garlicky smell of Jews in the tram — with head held high.

As the noose tightened, friends, one by one, departed for Palestine and America, but Gerda resisted the temptation to join them. Despite the strict quotas, she still hoped for a place at the university and, besides, she was needed at home to help care for her mother, suffering through the last stages of tuberculosis. When everyone, not just the young folks, began talking of emigration, havens had become harder to find.

At what point did she forget to think about Ludwig? Was it when she and her father walked in a daze down the platform at Union Station? It had been sheer luck that they got out when they did. They had been like all the other lost souls without papers, scurrying along the streets, ducking their heads when a Brownshirt appeared. Then, a miracle: a visitor's permit to England and, later, boat tickets to Canada from a cousin, Sheldon, in Toronto.

The last time they saw Ludwig, he was in his cellar flat

in Berlin, chain-smoking at the kitchen table, his blue eyes confused and sad. A brief, proud light flared in him when her father tried to persuade him to leave. He could not face more grovelling in the anterooms of consulates. He was determined to wait the Nazis out.

Somehow Ludwig slipped from her mind and, at that moment, it would seem, a cattle car slammed shut. Insane thought, outrageous and utterly symptomatic, according to the psychologists. She cannot bring herself to think beyond the slamming of the door. It shuts and her mind retreats and she is relieved by her lack of morbidity and she is aghast at her cowardice and it goes around and around. A textbook case. Still, she searches for the exact moment she forgot him. She recalls the old apartment on Bathurst Street, her father's bedroom and her own next door, where the radiators in winter gave off too much heat and she sat near an open window letting gusts of wind keep her awake.

She loved the lonely night hours. In those days Gerda Levittson, the medical student living in her father's house, itched for eleven o'clock, for the dreary Friday-evening Sabbath ritual to be over and for her father to plod down the corridor to his bed. Then, laying a towel along the bottom of the door to prevent light from spilling into the hall and arousing her father's peevish anger, she switched on the desk lamp. That fine, intense glare on the printed page. She tunnelled into the text, noted, memorized, added knowledge, brick by brick, to her solid foundations. The late-night stillness, immense and calm, buoyed her. She lifted her head from her books and felt it press against her. Solitude was a muscular embrace.

Friday nights in the Bathurst Street apartment. She and her father sat crowded amid the serving dishes in the dining room, which was cluttered with unnecessary sideboards and chairs. When did her father go back to the strict orthodoxy of his childhood? After the Red Cross telegram, or before? One day, when she had come back from a lab, a gleaming set of crockery, uncontaminated and ready for the new kosher regime, stood on the kitchen counter. A long list of injunctions went with it. On the Sabbath she was not to turn on a light, not to tear a page, not to put pen to paper, not to ride, not to carry any object — not even a book — outside the house. A prayer for rising and for lying down to sleep. A benediction for hearing good tidings and for hearing bad. A chain-link fence of rituals and commandments that invested the minutiae of daily life with enormous significance and kept everything outside at bay. The quaver in her father's voice as he laid down the law made her go along with it, while she planned her respites and escapes. How Ludwig might have teased and waggled a forefinger. She could hear his voice: "Have you said the benediction for slicing into a cadaver?"

Her father cooked and cleaned while Gerda went to her classes at the university. On Fridays she had to be home in time for the lighting of the candles. When she arrived he was wearing a velvet skullcap — special for *Shabbas* — on his bald, liver-spotted head and it made his jowly face look more withered and pathetic than ever.

He fussed, he shuffled between dining room and kitchen preparing the table — the two challah loaves and their cloth covers, the saltcellar, prayer book, dishes and cutlery. His aged hand held the *kiddush* cup in the air, the dark wine trembling at the brim as he recited the blessing in a gravelly voice. He did the *motzi*, blessing over bread. Slowly his stiff fingers tore off a piece of challah for her, sprinkled salt and placed it by her plate.

When she opened her mouth to say something, his hand flew to his face in an alarmed gesture. No talking between *kiddush* and *motzi*, she remembered. As she ate her salted bread, he hurried to the kitchen to bring out the meal. A pale chicken broth with bits of parsley and droplets of fat, just as his own mother used to make. Roast chicken, potato dumplings, peas and beets. The same dinner repeated itself every Friday, down to the canned dessert peaches and vanilla wafers, imported from Israel. He munched in silence, methodically, without a sign of pleasure or appetite. After sopping the last bit of gravy from his plate with his bread, he launched into a rambling monologue about arcane family customs.

"In your aunt's house they took their salt from a little crystal dish. Do you remember? No, you were too young. A silver-and-crystal dish, part of a set she had. They took a pinch between forefinger and thumb and sprinkled it on the challah. Like this, see? My mother thought it uncivilized, everyone dipping their fingers in the same dish. The thing is, now I don't know what is right...." His voice trailed off, thin and plaintive.

"Ask a rabbi," Gerda said, her eye on the clock.

"*Ach*, the rabbis here. Pollacks and Russians. They know things, of course. But it's not the same as a rabbi from home."

Finally, "Grace after Meals:" "...for your covenant, which you sealed in our flesh; for your Torah...for your laws...for life, grace and kindness...." His voice was a flat monotone.

He couldn't carry the tune at the singing parts, but did not seem to expect her to join in. At the last words he rapped on the table. *"Pflicht getan."* Duty done.

"Insomnia," she writes in her notebook, " is the most troublesome side effect. Medications: anti-spasmodic clonazepan (brand name Rivotril)...the tricyclic amitriptyline...a specialist from New Zealand prescribes an anti-convulsive...."

The group members are proud to have her in their midst. They look to her for answers. "I know nothing more than you do. There is little substantial research...." No matter. They describe symptoms and wait for her answers. Often she walks out of the meeting more dazed and battered than when she entered. Still she regards the meetings every second Thursday as a necessity. They are fellow shipwrecked travellers. They know, they hear. In their strained smiles and anxious eyes she sees the reflection of her own pain. It is as necessary to be in contact with them as to locate familiar objects in her room after troubled sleep. She envies them their simple-minded faith. They are eager to try herbal remedies, sound-masking devices, reflexology, colour therapy, acupuncture, although, from what Gerda can tell, the results of these treatments are highly inconclusive.

"Chronic *tinnitus* is chronic pain. Our nervous systems are not adapted to absorb the impact of a constant stimulus. Internally generated sound, from which there is no escape, creates an abnormal situation that can call forth the production of noradrenaline, a neuro-chemical that primes our responses...."

The nerve endings in the inner ear quiver. They cannot stop. The liquid around them is in perpetual motion.

One of the more bizarre theories to float out of the pages of the *Volkischer Beobachter* maintained that you could distinguish Jew from Aryan by the shape of the left ear. Ludwig snorted with delight when he read this. He had his photo taken in left profile and sent it, under the pseudonym Reiner Deutschmann, to the editor. An example of an impeccable Aryan ear. They printed it, with thanks. Ludwig was on top of the world.

The telegram from the British Red Cross was as brief and final as words on a tombstone. "Ludwig Levittson: last seen Berlin February 1943 boarding transport. Destination eastern territories. Regret no further information at this time." A scrap of newsprint paper with three badly typed lines, large "X"s over the mistakes and the date on top — September 5, 1946. The end of almost eight years of anxious inquiries, nightmarish rumours, a clutching at hopeful signs and growing certainty of doom. She put it in the file folder marked "Red Cross," which she slipped to the back of the drawer.

Her father had sat hunched at the end of his bed, his hands limp in his lap, tears dripping from his nose and chin. First he'd waved the brutal truth away. The telegram was vague, so sparse in detail. What kind of transport and which part of the East, could the Red Cross not find out, could it not have been possible....? Gerda shook her head, grim, determined to end this futile hanging on, this water torture of letters to officials and their carefully worded replies. Finally, he crumpled up and wept, resigned, helpless, exhausted, unrestrained.

While horrified at their abundance, Gerda envied him his simple flood of tears. It seemed he would cry the life out of himself. She stroked his shoulders and head, rocked him in her arms, averting her face from his wet, loose cheeks, his odour of age and despair.

As he wept, she planned the days ahead. Her first term of medical school was about to begin. She could not afford to miss a lecture, but could put off long study sessions for a couple of weeks while she kept him company until the worst was over. Then she must drive on with her own life's course.

During the months that followed, she prepared for mid-term exams. She ignored the silence that fell and the burst of chatter that rose up again like a wall when she walked into the med school cafeteria. All those male voices linked in camaraderie and common disdain. She bent her head, cheeks burning, toward her books.

At night, when her overcharged brain would not shut down, she would pick up the anatomy text at her bedside table. She'd trace the course of blood through the body, recite the soothing names of the heart's chambers: superior vena cava, inferior vena cava, atrium, atrio-ventricular valve. Aorta to arteries to minute capillaries where the blood cells push through, one by one by one, transform themselves through intricate chemical reactions, then carry on their timeless, perfect journey back to the heart.

Words roll and buckle on the page. Metal gates *crash*, *smash* against tender membranes already whipped raw. Noise is pain is noise and she is buried in it, six feet under, mouth, nose, ears stuffed with *smash*, *crash* and the *yowl* of the dead.

This is not madness, it's a condition, it's all the same.

"Enough now. Stop." Her frail, cracked voice takes aim at the bedlam. "Enough of this nonsense."

She reads aloud. She recites: "*Yitgadal v'yitkadash sh'mei raba....Im eshkachekh Yerushalayim*...If I forget you, O Jerusalem...." Whatever words come to hand until she stands solid again above the waves. "*Tinnitus*, from the Latin, meaning to ring or toll like a bell...."

The young ones these days don't know how to listen. Was she a good listener? Was she, really? She certainly knew how to translate the anguished, but vague, complaints into precise symptoms. The files on Mr. X grew fat. Symptoms noted, tests ordered, results collected, medications prescribed, side effects noted, medications changed.

Another scorcher, the radio announcer promises. The sky, glimpsed through the curtains of the kitchen window, has gone from black to milky grey. Streetlights wink, bring the daytime world into faint but unmistakable relief. Later on, the street will lie in dusty, yellow heat, but for now a pleasant breeze parts the kitchen curtains and caresses her face. The ocean roar is beginning to subside. Gerda sips scalding hot chamomile tea to soothe her stomach, which threatens to heave bile. Every bodily function now — a stubborn bowel movement, a fit of tears — can start up the tidal wave in her head. She takes small, wary sips. The stomach above all is a capricious beast that must be treated with respect.

Across the hall, she hears the soft click of a neighbour's door. Gerda opens her own door to greet Mrs. Paulsen, a pink-cheeked woman about Gerda's age, but younger looking, who is on her way to the garbage chute. Mrs. Paulsen's eyes, limpid and innocent, show that she takes the calm around her for granted. Her movements cause no reverberations. She could not imagine the shroud of echoes Gerda is buried beneath, although she has clicked her tongue and shaken her head over Gerda's ailments.

Back in the apartment, Gerda listens to the radio announcers, a man and a woman, who chatter about tie-ups on the 401 and a stalled truck that's spilled its load of hamburger buns onto the Don Valley Parkway. Morning sounds. A miracle of solid ground through the waves.

Who is she to deserve miracles?

She closes her eyes for just one instant, her attention wanders and look what happens. A row of naked, emaciated men totter above a ditch, topple down into the cold ooze, their mouths open but soundless, their eyes crying out in unspeakable horror. If she had kept that fine-tooled mind more alert, if she had listened for the clanging of the gate....

She continues writing: "Some people find relief through various treatments...masking devices that generate white noise...cassette tapes with the sounds of nature, ocean waves breaking on a shore."

There is no cure. Slowly, the mind flattens itself, adjusts, yields to the pounding wash. Slowly, sound and silence are one. A firmament appears in the midst of the waters.

In This Corner

Macho Man Randy Savage stomps down the aisle toward the ring, teeth bared, fists raised, mugging for the camera, hurling threats drowned out by the roaring crowd.

"More than 90,000 fans," bawls the announcer. "Madison Square Garden is packed." His voice is already hoarse and strained with excitement. Crank it up another notch and he'll lose it, Rachel thinks. He'll screech. He'll sound like the kind of candyass that Savage is vowing to bust into dust.

Her father sits perched on the couch in the shadows, bony legs crossed at the knees, chin in hand, a pose of mild contemplation. Rachel lingers by the basement entrance, trying to make out the grey blur of his face in the flickering light. He is thinner than he was the last time she saw him. Something to get used to with each visit home, this whittling away of age.

Upstairs pots and dishes clatter as her mother takes care of the aftermath of lunch. Saturday's "Raw Cuts" has become a ritual, the one sacred hour of the week. Eye on the clock as 1 p.m. approaches, her father hurries to clean his plate and shuffles downstairs, slippers flapping, into the gloomy darkness of the rec room.

"Go! Go to your fat men," Rachel's mother yells after him, but he pays no attention.

He waves the wand, steps back a pace at the blast of sound, then settles himself into his corner of the couch as Wrestlemania erupts onto the screen.

He could be studying Michelangelo's *David* the way he ponders, so sober and reflective. Or perhaps he's just absenting himself, using the noise and clamour on the set to mask his retreat into a distant and private place.

Macho Man leaps over the ropes and struts from corner to corner in his red body suit, black cape and jewel-studded cowboy hat. He howls. He rips off the brim of his hat with his teeth and tosses the pieces to the outstretched hands of adoring fans. Organ music swells as the opponent, Yokozuna, the Sumo wrestler, lumbers into view, a vat of a man, massive belly jiggling over his belt. The upward slant of his eyes is accentuated by black eyeliner. His hair is tied into a topknot. Ninety thousand "boos" rock the hall.

The men begin the careful, choreographed performance. They grunt, butt, sail into the air, *thud* down on the mat. They twist each other into impossible knots and pound the floor with feet and fists.

"How can you watch this stuff?" Rachel asks yet again.

"They're usually well-matched," her father says, slow and considering. "But I'm not so sure about today. It may not be a fair fight."

"But Dad, you can't still believe it's *real*."

Ernst Birnbaum. Eighty-one years old, spare and withered, five foot five in his down-at-the-heel slippers, 125 pounds and losing, slowly. Flesh has dripped away with the years, but the sober dignity in his features, the Old World cultivation, remains. A breeze of sidewalk cafés, onionskin newspapers, civilized pessimism wafts about his shoulders. All his life, the skeptic, the realist, embarrassed by displays of woolly sentiment. Even the singing of the national anthem in movie theatres used to make him twitch. A dry "we'll see" was all he had to say to Trudeaumania. And yet he was always so affected by the wounds of the smallest creatures. Rachel recalls the severed worm he found on one of their walks when she was a child. It returns in her dreams, raw and bloody, rising, quivering, falling to the sidewalk. He dropped her hand and lifted the thing between his forefinger and thumb to place it on the grass. She thrust her treasonous fists into her pockets, unable to grasp his worm-slimed hand again.

And now this. Macho madness, the roars and bellows, the sweat and spit.

A commercial break interrupts the action and Brutus Beefcake presses his face to the screen to tell fans about an upcoming match.

"I'm gonna squash his brains. You're toast, buddy. You're a Timbit. I'm gonna eat you for breakfast...."

"The whole thing is staged, Dad. It's so obvious."

He shakes his head and smiles almost sadly, as if she is the one harbouring illusions.

He still takes the train to the office in the mornings, but, once there, holds his head in his hands, watches from his backroom desk as Avi cuts the deals. He is tired. He has earned his tiredness, Rachel thinks. And his doubts. When Avi swings into the back room to tell him the latest — all their Sunseeker tours to the Caribbean booked, extra flights on order — his face wavers between pleasure and caution. For years he toiled away in the dusty one-room travel agency, transformed it finally, before Avi took over, into a plate-glass storefront on a minor downtown artery.

All his life hedging his bets, methodical and prudent, searching for some flat, narrow ground between extremes.

Macho Man moonsaults from the top of the ropes, but misses his opponent and seems to land on his head, which he holds and shakes as he stumbles to his feet.

"How can it be fake when you see what they do to one another?" her father asks, eyes still on the set.

"If it's real, how can you stand it?"

"But they're trained for it. And usually it's an even match." A grave nod. A dry little cough.

Rachel's mother thumps down the stairs and into the gloom of the basement. She wipes her dishwater-wet hands on her apron, glances at the screen, snorts with disgust.

"*Pfui*, those fat men, like slabs of beef."

"You're talking to the wall." Rachel moves over to where her mother is standing. She catches Hannah's eye and instantly they both hoot with laughter. They are weak with hilarity. Her mother's strained face becomes soft and warm, like a blanket shaken out in the sun.

"How they smack themselves around." Hannah wipes tears from her eyes.

"If you don't watch out he'll turn up the volume."

"Why can't he watch a *good* film, with me?" Hannah's tone changes. "Last night Greta Garbo was on and he leaves in the middle to go to bed."

Just as always. The ritual: her parents on the couch, Hannah at one end, Ernst at the other, washed in the glow of vintage black-and-white. Her mother sat engrossed. It was what Hannah wanted — a decent love story that dug deeply into the complexities of the human heart. Her father sat stiff and dutiful on his side for as long as he could stand it, then rose abruptly, pecked them both on the cheek and was gone.

And yet Hannah's complaints have lost their edge, have a resigned ring to them. The triumph of ridicule. The comfort of long-established routine, of knowing where to find him. In the old days, when Rachel still lived at home, the air snapped with bitterness, desire stifled.

It would start with a thread.

He sat in his armchair in the living room, stone-still, head slightly raised and eyes looking down through bifocals at the book held in front of him. Churchill's *History of World War II*. He was plodding his way through all six volumes, beginning with *The Gathering Storm* and ending with *Triumph and Tragedy*. Her mother, finished with the lunchtime dishes, crept down the hall to see if he was asleep. Finding him awake, she stood uncertain in the doorway. She watched for a moment, then plopped down in a chair opposite, heaving a sigh. Rachel, lying on the couch, allowed her own book to fall from her hands and met her mother's eyes, pulled despite herself toward Hannah's need. Her mother's hands flew palm-up in the air in a gesture of bewilderment, impatience, despair. *What do you want? Leave us alone*, Rachel said silently. She could not speak out loud, knowing how easy it was to tilt the equilibrium of the room, set off a string of explosions. Her father turned a page.

"Ernst, do you want a cup of tea?" Hannah's question sounded like a threat.

"Not now." His voice muffled and distant, as if coming from the bottom of a well.

"I want to show you my new dress now, all right? I need to know what you think."

A noise from his side of the room like a grunt, or a clearing of the throat.

She marched down the hall. Rachel could not help but listen for the squeak of drawers, the rustle of paper, the rattle of the mirror on the closet door. Eager, desperate sounds.

"Well, what do you think?"

She stood before him in a purple dress, hands fluttering, shoulders stiff, one higher than the other. It was always the same dress. A simple shirtwaist of cheap, shiny material bought at Ogilvie's bargain basement. Hannah's stomach pressed against the belt that accentuated her thickened waistline. He had given up trying to get her to spend money on more flattering clothes. He always met with unfathomable resistance.

"It's fine." His eyes flicked up and then down again.

"Look at me, for godsakes."

Churchill fell with a thud onto her father's knees.

"There's a thread hanging."

"Where, where?" She whipped around.

"There! There!" He bent down and jerked at the long wisp of purple that hung from her hem.

"You don't like it, do you? And now I can't give it back. But look at the colour. Look how nice."

His words came in an angry hiss that made Rachel shiver.

"It's the kind of dress women who clean toilets back home would wear."

Yokozuna lifts Macho Man above his head, shuffles around the ring with him as if he were a trophy and hurls him to the floor.

"*Sheeyah*, look at that," her father says, hugging himself.

Macho Man retaliates with a knuckle thrust to his opponent's eye, toppling him backward like a bowling pin. He grins, making hand-wiping gestures to the audience, while behind his back the Sumo wrestler climbs the ropes. The audience shrieks and groans, but it's no use. The brute drops ass-first onto his prey.

"*Ach*, poor guy. But what can you expect? An unfair match."

"*Pfuiyah*! Makes me want to vomit!"

"It's not real, Mum. It's all a show."

"What difference does it make? Come with me outside."

But Rachel lingers. She leans against the armrest of the couch letting the din of Madison Square Garden wash over her while Hannah clumps back up the stairs.

Yokozuna lifts Macho Man by his hair and the seat of his pants and *thunks* him headfirst against the ring post. Ninety thousand fans moan in protest, but Ernst is silent. She wonders if his interest is feigned after all. He refolds his arms across his chest, presses his cold hands into his armpits and continues to watch, or to dream, or to doze. It is easier for her to imagine the young man she never knew, the mist of possibilities he presents, than the father who sits beside her now, his long life wound up tightly inside him.

❧

He had told her often about his hometown, sometimes with nostalgia, sometimes with bitterness. He knew every back alley and every path in the adjacent woods. It was a famous spa town in western Bohemia with villas and cafés, hotels and promenades spilling up the sides of a valley tucked between steep, green hills. The centrepiece of the town was a hot spring that shot up 40 feet before collapsing upon itself, straining toward the ceiling of the glass hall that had been built around it. Visitors from all over Europe and America came to sip its salty, medicinal waters.

She had learned early on that Europe at that time had been like an elegant banquet table, covered with starched linen, laden with gleaming china and silver platters, but with a large hidden hole cut in its middle. Something evil waited underneath, tugging at the cloth. Anyone with his eyes open, he said, could see that a crash was coming.

One June day, while he stood on a curb sniffing the pine-scented air, a procession of brown-shirted men rounded the corner at the bottom of the street and marched toward him.

She imagines how it was. They sang as they approached, arms swinging, mouths falling open and shut. A song about verdant hills and the erasing of unnatural borders. Her father regarded their exalted, reddened faces, the suffocating intensity in their eyes. A few townspeople turned away, many others waved. Among the marchers he recognized an optometrist, a former school chum, several teachers from the high school, the owner of the hair salon on Schillerplatz. They moved forward, unselfconscious, as if pulled by a string. A young girl passed out flyers announcing a rally of the Sudeten German Party. He wanted to hurl himself against the line of forward-marching bodies, smash at least one of those upward-tilted chins against the curb. He wanted to roar out a string of obscenities. Instead, he pressed his lips together. He pulled himself up into a straight-backed, rigid stance, eyes fixed on the gilded clock face across the street.

Soon afterward, he left, marching toward the border with a small knapsack on his back. In the grey stillness of the morning, on the empty country road, he must have felt carefree as a child. He was alone in the immense, Godless silence. He had everything he wanted — a landscape large enough to disappear into.

But a few months later, loneliness pressed in as he lay on his cot in the kibbutz, surrounded by the yip and yowl of jackals. One evening he bowed to a young woman in a dance hall, a gesture so formal and eager, she burst into brilliant laughter. He was charmed by the reckless way she kicked up her heels while dancing the *hora*, her sudden red-faced awkwardness when a dress button came undone, how she fumbled with large, trembling fingers. He had wanted to protect, guide, enfold her.

When, then, did Hannah's need of him become a burden? Did he one day lean toward her intending a brief hug and find her arms locked around him? Did he pry her off as one might a child who makes a drama of going to bed?

Rachel remembers coming home to the bedroom door shut tight, a terrible silence behind it. Her father would be in his chair in the living room, facing Churchill. Hannah lay hunched up on the bed, face to the wall, as clay-heavy as the drowned. It was up to Rachel to effect her slow resuscitation. She touched Hannah's tear-stained face, stroked her hair, reasoned, encouraged, begged. Rachel's hands shook with tenderness and revulsion, with the need to pull her mother up from the deep and the temptation to push her further under. And where was he? If she could yank him from his chair, hurl him to his knees by the bed, if she could look him in the eye. But he had never turned on Rachel with that cold, annihilating stare that made her mother flail and scream. And she was not about to put him to the test.

The referee, absurd in his white shirt and bow tie, dances about, jabbing a finger in the air. Both men are on the floor, Yokozuna leaning over Macho Man with one great arm wrapped around his opponent's neck. They lie still for several seconds and it seems as if they've decided to take time out, but then a microphone picks up the whistle of breath and a sound like strangled retching.

Ernst looks up at her and smiles. He pats the couch beside him.

"Sit down, dear," he says and so she does, leaning her shoulder against him. He tucks her arm under his, as he used to do during their Sunday walks together.

It was always possible to achieve a truce. Sensing the moment, Rachel would take her mother's hand and lead her to where he sat. By then he would be uneasy and abashed, arms pressed against his chest.

"Well, then, shall we put this behind us?" he would say with a cough, as his eyes slid sideways. Not the tender reconciliation Hannah wanted, but a reprieve of sorts.

"I'm not the one who quarrelled." Her lame attempt to gain more of an apology from him.

He would rise, dart a kiss to the side of Hannah's head, her arms would encircle him, her tear-swollen face would press against his neck while he stood stiff, hands dangling. His eyes when they met Rachel's had a muddy, helpless look.

The crowd erupts. Waves of chanting. Ninety thousand voices knitted together. Both men are down again, writhing on the canvas. Yokozuna clasps his knee, Savage hugs his chest, while the referee cavorts around them, swinging his arm up and down as if clanging an invisible bell. Then, on cue, both men begin to stagger upward, shaking their massive heads. Sweat-drenched, reeling like drunkards, they collide once more and collapse onto the canvas.

"This is incredible, folks. The punishment these guys are taking. And they're getting up. I can't believe this. They won't give up."

It is *this*, Rachel realizes, her father is waiting for, what holds him here in this darkened, musty basement on a sunny afternoon. The sight of two punch-drunk hulks, blind with exhaustion and wrenched with pain, staggering to their feet. He leans forward, excitement flickers across his face. He grunts softly as his mind pushes upward, heaves against gravity along with Macho Man. His hands grope in the air, they miss and he must dodge, stumbling backward, in danger of being crushed one final, fatal time. He whirls around with a sudden burst of energy, hooks his arm under Yokozuna's armpit and does the impossible, heaves the massive body up, up and onto his shoulder, where it teeters, a mountain suspended in space. Then over and down to crashing defeat. Palms upraised in a victor's stance, he greets the thunderous applause.

"Ha, ha," her father says. His voice flies up an octave. "You see! You see!"

A Man Who Has Brothers

All that is still recognizable of Ernst Birnbaum is his ear. Erect and robust, gilded with the remnants of a Florida tan, standing at attention on his shrunken head. It is turned toward Rachel as she gazes down at her father in the hospital bed. She'd know that ear anywhere. The rest of him is a wasted fetal form, limp and grey-skinned. Unbelievable this process, how each day he dissolves more, each day he is less distinguishable from the grey-green hospital gown, veteran of a thousand launderings.

Rachel touches the rim of her father's ear with her fingertips. Cold. But ears usually are. She brings her mouth close. Supposedly hearing is the last sense to go.

"Papa, it's me, Rachel. Your *Rachele. Papa, Ich bin da.*" Useless words. As useless as the colourless fluid that, until a few days ago, dripped from a plastic pouch above his head through a tube into his veins and through another tube out again. "I'm here. I love you. I'm Rachel." Repeated and redundant, swallowed up in the cavern of his mind. Cold breath on congealing waters.

Days ago he was still responding, could mumble a few words and his hand in hers could answer with gentle pressure. Lifetimes ago, she was still able to rush around and find ways to bring comfort. While her mother hung over the steel railing of his bed, awkward, trembling, dangerously unbalanced, or stood stricken in the corridor outside his room, Rachel dashed through streets and shopping malls, returning quickly, quickly, with a duck-down quilt from home, a portable radio/ tape player with earphones, giant-size Kleenexes, a large-faced wall clock. She manoeuvred the car through city traffic only to fret at the interminable, ungodly tie-ups in the hospital parking lot. Incredible. A man wastes away to a skeleton, his heart knocks against his ribs with a cold that thin hospital blankets do nothing to mitigate, yet the lot attendant yawns. The ticket machine sticks out a blue tongue. The swing arm creaks up, lets a car inch forward, creaks down.

She tucked the quilt around him. She fed him Strauss waltzes through the earphones of the portable player. She mounted the wall clock because he could no longer see the thread-thin hands of his wristwatch and because a nurse suggested it would help ground him to know the time of day.

One time she found him restless, moaning, while one arm groped feebly toward the lower half of his body. She rushed to the bed, called out to him and he froze, then went still, so that at first she thought she'd woken him from a fitful sleep. He remained too quiet though, breathing with obvious care, his brow furrowed.

"What is it, Papa? Should I call the nurse?"

He took no notice of her for several moments, then gave a weak smile and shook his head, but his eyes remained guarded and distant. She felt awkward. Had she stumbled in on a private moment? She realized how exposed he must feel with his suffering so close to the surface.

"Are you all right dear?"

Nurse Judy Kimber, blond and rosy and uniformed in pink, slips into the room, then, with a pat to Rachel's shoulder, out again. A good 10 years younger than Rachel and calling her "dear," but with no disrespect intended. Rachel has heard Judy call her father "sweetie" and "darling" as she cradled his head in her hand, feeding him broth. This is the oncology ward, such excesses are normal. Judy is a candy-coloured angel.

The second hand jerks forward. The second hand jerks forward — 4:34 and 28 seconds. Pain has subsided. Silence bears down on the dimly lit room. Nevertheless his ear beckons, open, receptive, a cup into which she could pour, what? Confessions, secrets, a final revelation, a magical promise? If only she had one.

His own revelation flew at her one day. It beat her face with black wings, then disappeared, dissolved into an ordinary, blue September sky.

They were sitting on a park bench together looking across Lac St. Louis as it winked and danced in the sun. How did he get to be so old, so collapsed into himself, she wondered. Retirement was to blame. He shouldn't have stopped going to the office, even if it was just to put in time. Now he rose late in the morning, shined his shoes as always, but left them on a sheet of newspaper by the back door while he shuffled about in worn slippers, wandered to the living room window to stare at the empty street that was frozen in mid-week tranquillity. She and her brother Avi were scheming, though, to get him into a retirement village in Florida. Golden Gate Resort. She had the brochure in her purse: a community of whitewashed condominiums surrounding an artificial lake and groomed lawns, with a tuckshop, a pool, activities.

Her father had leaned against her slightly on the bench, flicked peanut crumbs from his pocket at approaching sparrows.

"Great day," she ventured.

"*Ach ya*, beautiful." He shook his head and sighed at this beauty, amazed or bewildered by it, or perhaps doubting it would last.

"What would you like to do next, Papa? What have you always dreamt of doing, but didn't get around to?"

Sparrows fluttered in the dirt at their feet. Waves lapped the shore. The factory smokestacks across the lake barely smudged the air.

"I should have gone to Auschwitz," he said in a slow, flat voice as if commenting on the probability of rain. "I had the chance a few years ago when I was in Europe, but I didn't have the nerve."

She had never heard him pronounce the name before. The profanity, uttered in her father's cultured German. She stared at an object far out on the lake, perplexed as to whether it was a buoy or a duck.

"When were you in Europe?" she said at last. She could not recall him having gone anywhere for years, other than to trundle back and forth to Montreal by commuter train.

"We were in Switzerland, don't you remember? Our walking holiday in Arosa? Your mother's old friend, Gerda, came to join us for the last week and I said I had to get back early because of business. I had it all planned. They stayed behind

142

at the *pension* and I took the train to the airport in Zurich. I had a visa for Poland; I was on my way. But I couldn't go through with it." He shook his head, picked at a thread on his buttonhole with thin, dry fingers.

She was stunned that he had taken the plan so far. She felt a childish pang of betrayal as she imagined him setting out, disconnected from all of them, rushing toward an alien land.

"Actually, what happened was, I got a migraine like I hadn't had for years."

She could understand why he'd try to slip away without her mother knowing. A tour of ovens and gas chambers? Hannah wouldn't have allowed it. All that money, pristine mountain air, exercise and good food, blown away.

"I should have done more to save my family. I know it makes no sense," he said, turning a bitter smile upon her. "But it goes through my head. Perhaps I could have done something. I think of it every day."

What family, she almost said. It had been so long since he'd mentioned them.

"But what could you have done?"

"I know."

The moment stretched out between them. She searched the lake for the buoy or the duck, a black dot that dipped, disappeared and reappeared. She took a deep breath.

"You're not getting out enough, Papa. You're too isolated and the winter will be worse. A month from now, you won't even be able to come to the park."

She pulled out the brochure and explained how easy it would be, how little it would cost. Forty dollars a day for the two of them, including car rental. She pointed out the nature sanctuary nearby and read the description. "A biologic wonderland where visitors are rewarded by sights of alligators, rare plants, unusual animals, odd and beautiful birds."

He stared at a picture of a wood stork, perched on a branch. It was not the most beckoning sight, Rachel realized, with its naked neck and head, dark wrinkled skin and ungainly bill. Freakish.

"*Ach ya,*" he sighed. "It's an idea. I have to think about it." His voice trailed off. He plunged his hands between his crossed legs to warm them. He turned suddenly and lifted her chin toward him in the old way, brow knitted with concern.

"You look pale. Are you getting enough fresh air?"

"I'm fine, Papa. Healthy as a horse. Anyway, I do aerobics twice a week."

They rose to stroll arm in arm along the lakefront, his step still light and firm, although he wheezed and snuffled, dabbed every few moments with his handkerchief at the perpetual drip at the end of his nose.

"*Ach*, nonsense," her mother said later when Rachel told her about the conversation in the park. "He doesn't dwell on the past. He's a sensible man. We all lost family. It was a long time ago."

Family had always meant the four of them — Papa, Mama, Avi and herself — self-contained, unbreakable as an atom despite the small daily explosions. There were a few relatives in faraway places – England, the States — whose pale blue air letters arrived in the mailbox at holidays and birthdays and who were names with well-worn stories attached to them, but not faces. There were dead ones too, she knew that, but had no grasp of who they were. They were nameless, once-upon-a-time people, faint as shadows on an almost overcast day. A familiar, comfortable absence.

Once, when she was quite young, she heard her father utter the words, "My brothers."

Rachel was at an age when curiosity was an itch. She sensed mysteries all around her, treasures in the hidden spaces between the couch cushions. Her hands crept into drawers. Her finger poked through the torn vinyl of the kitchen chair, into the depths of its stuffing. She pricked up her ears when her parents talked in low voices, half in English, half in German. An endless drone of meaningless grown-up talk, yet sometimes magic happened. Two words leapt hard and bright out of the fog. "My brothers."

"What brothers?"

Silence in the kitchen. Her parents shifted in their chairs. They looked at one another.

"Tell me. Tell me."

Her mother jumped up, got the chocolate pudding out of the fridge and scooped a shivering heap into a glass dish. Cool and slippery on the tongue. Rachel lost her question in its sweet, yielding texture.

In bed at night, though, the words came back to her. She had a brother, Avi. Her friends had brothers whom they bullied and bickered with, or who tagged along. But that was different. Her father was a grown-up. And unlike any other grown-up, he was usually alone, in his chair with the newspaper or a fat book, on the balcony, staring out across the roofs of neighbouring houses. And even when he played checkers with Avi or herself, shaking his head with wonder at their clever moves, or when he lifted his head from his bowl of soup to tell the story of the *nudnik* client at the office, his tongue lolling to make them laugh — even then, his eyes seemed quietly elsewhere. His aloneness was sturdy and reassuring, companionable and undemanding, like the lava-black rock that jutted up from the ground in the nearby woodlot, giving Rachel the perfect all-season perch.

Such a man did not have brothers.

❧

The itch got her into trouble.

She had climbed out of bed to get a glass of milk, walked into the living room where her father sat alone on the couch — a blur in the grey wash of TV light. From down the hall came the splash of water, her mother having a long soak in the tub.

"What are you doing up?" He squinted at her through the flickering glow.

"I'm thirsty."

"Well, hurry up."

When she came back he was leaning forward, hugging himself with his hands in his armpits. On the screen she saw a puppet in striped pyjamas reeling from side to side, but she could not see the strings that held it up. She rested her shoulder against the living room archway and lifted her glass to her lips.

"Get out!"

She had never heard his voice like that, a sharp-toothed edge to it. He was on his feet, waving his arms and still she couldn't see his face in the gloom. She froze for a moment, then for some reason dodged around him, deeper into the living room, still clutching her glass, trapped by this stranger.

"Didn't I tell you to get out!"

She stepped backward, almost bumped into the TV behind her and turned around. It was not a puppet, it was a skeleton man and he was running forward with his arms raised.

A hand smacked across her thighs. Milk flew from the glass onto the carpet. As she ran from the room, the injustice of it crashed down on her. She had done nothing. The milk on the carpet was *his* fault. She stood in the kitchen, heart thumping, waiting for him to come after her. But he didn't.

A few minutes later she heard tinkling voices — her favourite commercial. "E-N-O, when you're feeling low, ENO!" And then he called out over the singing voices, "You can come in now." He patted the couch beside him, tousled her hair when she sat down. They watched in silence through several more commercials — Rothman's, Brylcream, Colgate with the Gardol Shield. When the news came on he tapped his watch.

"Off to bed," he said in his mock-horrified voice.

When he finally did offer bits of stories she was only half listening. His brothers, their wives and one child, Louisa, stayed behind in Europe. They all perished in the war. She knew the brother's names — Thomas and Martin — though not the names of their wives. Who was the older, who the younger, she could never remember. They were both much older than her father, born in 18-something while he — as he liked to point out — was a child of the 20th century. They lived in an ancient Bohemian town near Prague, with castles and mansions, red-roofed houses strung along a river, churches for a multitude of saints and a lone

147

synagogue, all enfolded by blue-green, forested hills. The brothers had a store on the arcaded promenade, where they sold beautifully made shoes from Italy and Prague. Birnbaum and Sons.

He liked to talk about the town. Not about its inhabitants or history, but about the woods he'd roamed and about the quality of its air, that forest-and-stream-filtered air that rolled down from the hills and up again.

She remembers the ritual Sunday-morning walks of her childhood in Montreal, how they would stop to catch their breath after a long scramble up the twisted paths of Mount Royal and how he would sniff the air, perhaps give it a passing mark. She remembers how he looked in those days: neat, dignified, handsome, with his thick, trained-back hair, short-sleeved white shirt, suit jacket slung over his shoulder and, of course, his flawless leather shoes, buffed to a high gleam that morning even though they would soon be covered with dust.

The point of the story of Thomas and Martin, she used to think, was her father's survival, not their demise. He got out because he was the youngest, the luckiest, the dreamiest, the one with the least to lose, the one with the least head for business. His escape from danger gave her wings, made her own life inevitable. Was that not what his reassuring nods over the newspaper, and his silence over the disappeared, had meant?

The family photo albums were almost entirely filled with pictures of her and Avi, their baby, toddler and school years in a parade of Kodak glossies interrupted only occasionally with a shot of her parents in Palestine. But in a bottom drawer, in an envelope, under a pile of old bills, cracked and grainy faces must have lain in wait. She thinks she has seen...but no, those were faces in museums, documentary black-and-whites of hollow eyes and grim mouths.

The couple with their daughter Louisa escaped to Prague, did they not? They hanged on doors in the middle of the night, seeking refuge. Or maybe that was another story altogether.

She thinks she remembers his voice, flat and final, saying, "Yes, I was lucky. While my brothers perished."

At some point, she had stopped asking. Because she had secrets of her own, because of the unbearable withdrawal in his eyes, because she had forgotten the question.

Why did people say "perished" or "lost in the war" rather than "died" or "killed"? If you were lost, you could be found again. Is that what they meant?

"I had an uncle," Hannah told Rachel one day. They were sitting on her parents' patio overlooking the back lawn, bright with sunshine.

"Uncle Morris. A kind man and a *bon vivant*. Not so religious as my father. He went to his favourite alehouse every Saturday for herring and beer. He was big and fat and loose, but always dressed just so in a three-piece suit with a gold watch chain dangling from his waistcoat pocket and a carnation in his lapel. My aunt Ida put a fresh one in every morning. Uncle Morris loved fine clothes, good food and especially his schnapps. He was fat, but light on his feet. He sailed across the dining room, unstopped the crystal decanter, poured himself a glass and brought it to his nose. Such a performer. And then the way he smacked his lips and let out a big, wet 'ahhh.'

"We would follow him around and imitate him. Partly laughing at him, yes, such monkeys, but partly just loving the sound he made. That 'ahhh!' He put his guts into it and it sent a thrill up your spine, like a note in an aria. We wanted to do it too, but of course we couldn't. We sounded like sick cats, strutting about, patting our stomachs.

"Anyway, poor Morris went insane shortly after he arrived at Auschwitz." She lowered her voice, spoke in a rush, although there was no one else around.

"I heard about it from a second cousin I met on the streets of Tel Aviv after the war. He saw them beat his Ida with whips. Who knows what for, she was half dead already. A day later, I think, he tore off his prison uniform — cap, shirt, pants, the works — and ran naked to the latrine, the stinking, overflowing latrine and rolled around...."

She stopped to take a breath. Her chest heaved under her apron.

"Anyway, the point is, that's not what I think about. I think of Morris in his dining room, with his thick fingers holding the schnapps glass like it was a flower."

"Come," she said, rising abruptly. "Come see my hedge roses."

Rachel followed her mother, who walked with arthritis-stiff and determined steps, to the trellis by the back fence. Most of the blossoms were past their prime, brown at the edges, but some were still unblemished, bursts of creamy white against green. She raised a flower, not to her nose, but to her mouth and turned her head from side to side to let the cool petal stroke her lips.

Thomas and Martin. She speaks their names. Speaks them out loud with the German accent that her father would use. She sees nothing. Feels nothing. They are lost.

The second hand jerks. It is neither dark nor light, day nor night. Her father still breathes yet seems utterly still. She has risen and fallen on the tiny sea of his chest for so long, she has lost all sense of motion.

"Take a break, dear."

Judy, the pink-clad nurse, glides noiselessly to the bed, checks a plastic bag of fluid waste that drains from his body. A perfunctory check. Her job is nearly done.

Rachel gropes toward the hallway. It's long after visiting hours, yet the hall seems crowded and humming. Colours jump out at her: the lemon-yellow of the walls, the lime-green trim, the metallic gleam of instruments on a trolley.

One of the patients, an old man in a plaid robe, shuffles out of his room pushing the IV tower before him. She has seen him often. He has a kicked-in-looking face, wrinkle-scored and bruised, and bird's nest eyebrows. A few weeks ago he would have seemed pathetic with his trembling shoulders and painful progress. Now he seems a miracle. He can stand. He can walk. One slippered foot in front of the other, he will make it all the way down to the lounge. She moves with him. Feels the polished floor under his feet, the rush of air, hot stabbing in his lungs. His green plaid slippers match his robe. Someone — perhaps he, himself — still cares about appearances.

How long since her father last wore shoes? He fell in a downward spiral from slippers to socks stretched over edema-swollen feet to nothing at all.

He always took special care of shoes. The Birnbaum and Sons slogan was: SHOES TO LAST A LIFETIME. Once he could afford it, he bought quality — rich, soft leather, solidly stitched. He polished religiously. Sunday mornings, before breakfast, he stood in the doorway of the back fire escape, the family's footwear lined up on newspaper in a neat row. He slipped a shoe over his left hand, examined the week's damage and began the reparations. With an old sock on his right hand, he daubed polish over the surface of the leather, rubbed firmly into every seam and crack, let the shoe stand to dry, then buffed with a brush. The hallway smelled of Cat's Paw polish and damp air from the courtyard below.

He scolded her when he caught her cramming her feet into her shoes without untying the laces. "Show some respect for what was once alive. That is the skin of an animal."

In the armchair near her father's bed, she dreams she is wrapped in a plaid robe with an IV tube protruding from her navel. She takes the tube between thumb and forefinger and aims it at a blank television screen across the room. She points and squeezes, squeezes and points, but nothing happens.

Waking, she remembers a picture of a mountain of shoes. It's in a book she's been reading on and off for the past month. She keeps it buried at the bottom of her suitcase and sneaks it out when she hears her mother settle down in the room next door. Men's, women's, children's. Boots, sandals, loafers, ordinary walking shoes. Thrown pell-mell into the heap, not a pair to be seen, all singles. Mashed down, crushed, battered, all a dull, uniform mud colour. A museum exhibit. Confiscated from the prisoners in Majdanek, reads the caption.

How long since she last saw her father's feet? His body is a faint "S" beneath the blanket. Nestled together, his limbs take up little space. Breath seeps in and out, washes over beached lungs. The ear seems to detach itself and hover.

Let me go in your place. I'll go there for you. I'll bear witness. Let me.

Surely he must hear.

Mother Tongue

I want her to tell me a story. One of those old German fairy tales that she loves so much and used to read to me as I lay in her bed, half sick with a cold, half faking it so that we could both stay home wrapped in the feather comforter and make believe. *Mother Holle*. How did it go? A good girl and a bad girl. The good girl shook Mother Holle's feather-bed, made it snow, and a shower of gold coins rained down upon her. The bad girl disobeyed and was smothered in pitch.

It had snowed outside our house as she read aloud. Fat, feathery snowflakes brushed against the window, danced down, drew us up into the spilled-milk sky.

Do you remember *Mother Holle*, I will ask, as soon as she wakes from the codeine-laced stupor for which I am responsible. Her head lolls back on the deck chair, her mouth gapes open and sucks in humid, lung-clogging Florida air. The sky above our screened lanai is shimmery grey, dull and bright at the same time. It stabs the eyes. Everyone, everything, at Golden Gate Resort is quiet and hunkered down in the afternoon heat. Palm trees droop. The gecko on the railing has turned to wood.

She tried to read to me long after I was old enough to read for myself. I wanted stories in English then, the language of the *real* world. *Little Women, Black Beauty, Nancy Drew*.

And to read in my *own* bed, in the early morning before any one else was up. She wanted to cuddle me against her pillow-soft breasts and read in her hushed voice, almost crying the words: "What are you afraid of, *mein Kind*? I am Mother Holle. I will do you no harm...." She turned the pages with trembling fingers. Age-softened, yellow-spotted pages with engravings of castles, gnarled trees, porridge pots, long-toothed witches. Later, I had words to explain what she was: a Romantik, a German *Romantik*, written with a "k." Simmering with *Weltschmertz* and longing for a wild-wooded, pure-aired, prewar, preindustrial Germany that never was. What an absurd position, Mother, what quicksand to stand on for a Jew.

I wanted to get her a wheelchair. Just for a few days so that I could take her on excursions along the beach boardwalk and the mile-long path that circles Golden Gate Lake. She could gaze upon the mint-cream sea, the misted sky, sandpipers, pelicans, hibiscus blooms in cocktail colours. But she wouldn't allow it, prefers to walk on her own two swollen feet, rusty joints, ravaged knees, ground-down hips. She prefers to fight the searing arthritis that was supposed to dissolve in the Florida sun. Leaning on her walker, she thumps down on her good leg, swings around the bad one that hangs from her side like an anchor in mud. Long, muffled moans, trickles of sweat on her seamed neck beneath the wide-brimmed hat and between her hunched shoulders. She inches forward. If she were in a wheelchair I could push her around the lake to the bridge she loves, where she could look down and see the turtles and ducks.

I shuffle beside her at her geriatric pace and plot another battle: a warm bath; a nice rest on the lanai, legs elevated; two extra-strength Tylenol with codeine. She shouldn't wait for the pain to get so bad that she'd need twice the recommended dosage. I would go to Publix myself for the groceries, spare her the crowded aisles, the blasts of icy air spewing out of vents and freezers.

But she insists on coming too. She staggers along, draped over the shopping cart, still dazed after a bad night's sleep and the morning's medication. She lingers at the produce department, eyes brightening over the heaps of melons, grapefruit, pineapples, mangoes. She weighs oranges in her palms, brings a yellow-skinned plum to her nose, leaves her shopping cart and lurches toward the strawberry sale while my back is turned. I see her stumble and catch herself just in time.

I steer her over to the bread department, last item on our list. Her eyes roam over shelves and shelves of bagels, Italian bread, Polish rye, egg loaf, seven-grain, but none of them are what she wants. None "real bread." Her complexion is weary grey. She hangs over the cart.

"Mama, *komm schon*. Come on. Just take something."

She prods a packaged loaf with her finger. "*Wiederlich*! Clings to the roof of your mouth and gives you heartburn."

"Mama, I've had it."

The woman in the yellow tank top examining dinner rolls looks up and smirks, looks down again. Does she know German? Or is it just my universal, exasperated-daughter voice?

"Don't talk so loud," I hiss, as I push my mother toward the cash.

ॐ

I have plans for our week together. I've come equipped. In the side pocket of my suitcase I've got a tape recorder and a five-pack of 90-minute, low-noise tapes. I want to know about my grandmother who died in the Spanish flu epidemic of 1919, leaving my mother motherless, about my grandfather and his love for Torah and the German Kaiser. About the town she grew up in that no longer exists. It's a Polish city now — everything that would have been familiar to her, everything German or Jewish, expelled, 300 years of history extinguished.

Stretched out on the deck chair, she sleeps the sleep of the battle-worn, at rest except for her tremor-ridden hand, which dances a mazurka in her lap. The screened lanai enfolds us in bug-free shade.

She wakes, groggy and confused. A flash of pain shoots back into her eyes.

"I saw a snake. There are snakes in the water."

"No, no Mother. There are no snakes here."

She points. Golden Gate Lake lies still, ringed by clipped lawns and cream-coloured condos. A man-made lake with all the original swamp dug out of it.

"So many snakes. Long black snakes."

Golden Gate Resort is plastic-wrap pristine. No pests here, no cockroaches or ants even. They are blasted away every Tuesday by men in green overalls wielding spray guns. My stomach jumps. What's happened to her mind? Pain and medication have short-circuited the wires, leaving a babbling stranger.

She presses her knuckles into her side, smiles up at me through a sigh and the abyss recedes. She is back.

"Where does it hurt, Mama?"

"Here. No, here and here mostly." Her hands skim thighs, knees, rib cage, belly. "I don't know. It moves."

"I'll get you some mint tea."

Put on the kettle. Find another cushion for her legs. Turn off the fan; she mustn't get chilled. Check if it's time for her next round of medication. Stow the suitcase, tape recorder and tapes out of the way.

I will splash warm water over her legs to soothe aches lodged in bone. I will catch the pain dragon by the tail. It leaps quickly from joint to joint, limb to limb.

I grasp her under the arm, hold her steady, my naked mother. "Careful. Put your hand on the grab bar. That's it."

She lies back in the water, a tired old sack, gnarled feet, bloated belly. Yet despite the wrinkles and age spots, her skin is surprisingly soft and a fine, pale gold. I am awestruck still, uncovering her nakedness.

She shrieks as I sponge her sides.

"That tickles."

She laughs, catches me with her laughter, hauls me along until we're both on this wild ride, unable to stop, doubled over. I fall onto the wet, tiled floor.

"Stop. Stop. I'll never get you out of that tub."

I realize later that she had seen long, black, curved necks stretching out of the water — the anhinga, also known as the water turkey. A common Florida bird, not a snake.

We go by car to Knippels, the German delicatessen in an arcade of boutiques on Fifth Avenue.

"I have a surprise for you, Mama."

A smile dawns as she peers at the windowpane, at Gothic script and painted dwarfs on the glass, red-capped, grinning, bearing between them a huge brown loaf on a board. More kitsch in the display case beyond — glazed dough figures of Hansel and Gretel in front of a gingerbread witch's cottage, a doll-size oven, miniature brooms.

I help her manoeuvre the walker around the glass door and into the store, which is cool and smells like fresh-baked heaven. She eyes the shelves of crusty loaves and rolls.

"See Mama, this is where you can get your real bread."

She leans toward a small loaf of black pumpernickel and sniffs. Then she notices the price.

"*Verruckt*, crazy," she says indicating the tall smiling man behind the counter. "It costs $3.95 American for this?"

"What do you want? It's a specialty shop."

"*Der Gauner.* Thief," she mutters.

"Shh. He'll understand."

"*Frisch*," says the storeowner. "Baked an hour ago." His smiling face looks like it, too, just came out of the oven. Brick-red cheeks. Small, blackcurrant eyes.

"How much for this?" she asks in her rough-hewn English.

"*Drei Dollar, fünfundneunzig, bitte.*" Still smiling and inviting chat in their native tongue. Chat that would lead to embarrassing questions. (Where in Germany are you from? When did you come to America?)

"You said $3.95?" It's an accusation more than a question and at his nod her hand begins to sink under the weight of the overpriced loaf. I toss exact change onto the counter and grab her arm.

The sweet aroma of warm bread fills the car. She stares at the dashboard, her face a battleground — anger, longing, suspicion, need.

We are surrounded by Germans. Young couples with children. Small groups of pensioners. They are indistinguishable from the parade of other tourists with their bland, cheery faces and their Bermuda shorts, matching tops, sparkling white Nikes, except when they open their mouths, call out *"Jawohl,"* *"Guten Tag,"* jolting me with their strange-familiar utterances. This resort town on the Gulf Coast is a favourite destination for tour operators in Hamburg, Cologne, Berlin, all those rich cities well padded in Deutschmarks that go so much further than our miserable Canadian dollars. The German tourists are interspersed among the throngs of silver-haired snowbirds from the northern states and Canada. She drops her voice as we sit and chat on the boardwalk and the crowd streams by.

With my father I speak English, but my mother and I have always spoken German together, laced with smatterings of Yiddish, Hebrew, English, my own bastardizations, our coinages and play words, endearments, quips and phrases repeated over decades. Our private, intimate language. Her mother tongue and mine, although I butcher the grammar. It's my bedtime-story, kitchen-table language. I leave it behind the moment I leave her. I speak it with no one else. Ours is a country with a population of two.

It was a shock to me when I first realized that other people spoke German too. I hid my knowledge of their language, preferring to let them approach me in English, a tongue that is cool, neutral, safe. I still do.

The checkout counter at Wal-Mart. A dark-haired woman about my own age behind me.

"Exyoose me," she says with a tentative smile. "Do you know ver zer iss a post office?"

A split second in which to decide. I speak slowly, so that she will understand, but allow a fake American drawl to creep into my voice. Anything more is a minefield, leads to false claims, assumptions of a common bond. It's not *her* language I speak.

I am awkward in our mother tongue, but she is hilarious, emphatic, bold. Her lips part and out fly a flock of indignant sounds and crazy combinations. *"Abscheulich!" "Unerhört!" "Es ist zum kotzen."*

She opens her mouth and out sails a song.

She used to sing in the kitchen in the morning before the rest of us were up. Hands sunk in dumpling dough — mashed potato, flour and egg — her deep voice boomed out Schubert and Mozart and simple melodies with rocking-horse rhymes. *"Lieder...wieder...flieder...."*

It's been years now since she stopped singing, though she'll hum sometimes or whistle under her breath. A sighing sound like a dying wind.

Her English was uncooked dough in her mouth. It stained my childhood with foolish shame. I hid behind the cornflakes boxes as she asked questions of the smirking Steinbergs boy, his face half turned away. "Pleece. How much iss ziss?" "Your epples, are zey goot?"

We spoke German together in the aisles, attracting a few over-the-shoulder glances but not the stares that her twisting and wrenching of English words would elicit. We chatted, incomprehensible and therefore invisible, our voices blending with the clatter of the cash register.

She used to have a ritual she called "twilight hour". I would come home from school in the afternoon to find the living room rearranged. The armchairs would be pulled close to the big picture window, curtains pinned back for an unobstructed view of the maple tree, its bare branches spread against the grey winter sky. The coffee table proffered tea, chocolate mousse, tangerines. The radio poured forth Vivaldi. Something for each of the senses. Her aunt Ida had started the tradition, inviting her nieces to join her by the window overlooking gabled roofs and church spires. They sat in straight-backed chairs and recited poetry until the last of the daylight drained from the sky.

Mother wanted to read to me from her old book with the yellowed pages and the cracked spine that dropped dried glue crumbs on the table. The book wasn't from before the war — she had nothing at all from that time. She'd found it in an antiquarian bookstore on Mansfield Street. Poetry and tales from the *Romantik* era, printed in heavy Gothic script that, for me, evoked fortresses, dungeons, iron bars, marble tombs. She read in a singsong voice, emotion bubbling close to the surface, the beauty of the words threatening to push her over the edge into absurd exaltation.

I wanted to mock her. Instead I did research. I scoured the reserve stacks at the public library for books on anti-Semitism, German nationalism, and discovered faint but perceptible arrows leading from *Sturm und Drang*, to *Romantik*, to Hitler.

"Open your eyes," I said. "A nasty epithet, a vile couplet, in the works of every one of your beloved authors."

"There was greatness as well," she said. "You can't dismiss a whole culture."

"Look here," I said, producing a verse by Wilhelm Busch, the humorist she quoted daily. " 'See the Jew with crooked nose and crooked soul....' "

"And Shakespeare? And Dickens?"

And all those Fatherland-loving Jews carted to the camps?

I switched on the standing lamp. It threw its light around the room and blotted out the fading dusk.

The language of Gestapo commands, camp regime, words that flail at cowering heads. *Raus! Aufstehen!* Words sharp and precise, slicing off the mother tongues of millions. *Judensau. Scheissjude.* Taunts that root and exult and wallow in filth.

Twilight hour on the lanai. Pain has abated for the moment. She sits leaning forward, good hand clenched around the other's trembling fingers, peering at the orange streak of sky above the Australian pines. A string of pelicans sweeps down low over the lake, wheels above our heads, then up and away. Her face softens in the evening light, sheds decades. Beyond our line of vision the Florida sun plunges into the sea. Shadows deepen. Orange fades to black. Night swallows day. TV screens and floodlights take over.

She comes to me in the middle of the night. I feel her breath on my face and the bed heave as her dead weight drops beside me.

"I can't sleep," she sobs. "The pain."

I leap up and away.

"I'll get you the Tylenol. I think you can have another one now." The digital clock on the bedside table says it's 3:23.

"No," she moans. "It makes me sick to my stomach."

"I'll call the hospital."

"Just let me lie here beside you for a while." She tucks her feet under the rumpled sheet. Her face blends with the shadows, her body looms large and clammy with sweat under her brushed-nylon nightgown.

"You go back to sleep," she whispers. "I'll be very still."

I switch on the table lamp and she stares up at me with tormented, pleading eyes. She shuts them again, as if guessing how they jeopardize her chances.

"Mama, I really should...."

"All I want is to lie here. Is that too much for a mother to ask?"

I switch off the light and lie down on my back beside her, stiff, hands folded on my stomach, holding myself as separate as possible and yet feeling the invasion of her sweat, her restlessness.

When I was a little girl, she begged in laughing tones, "Do *krabbele, krabbele* in my hair" and I played with her stiff thick locks imagining my fingers marching through a forest.

She looms all around me. I lie still, pretending to sleep, and so does she, it seems, until I hear a rumble beside me, sound of a plough pushing gravel. I pull the sheet up around her, slip out of the room and to the living room couch, which is safe and narrow and admits only one.

She used to come into my room after the lights were out when I was much too old to be checked on or tucked in. The obscene creak of floorboards announced her hand on the doorknob, so careful yet relentless, turning, opening. She burst in on my cave-world, my dreams of mouths and kisses, my body rocking, my hand probing. I lay still. She crept in, knelt down, her eyes boring into the dark with love and loneliness and fear.

"*Mein Kind*, my treasure," she breathed into the blankets, while I made my chest rise and fall in a steady, untouchable, clock-ticking rhythm.

Something loomed above my head. Her hand moved closer, tentative, touched the outer layer of my hair. She stroked the air around me, so careful yet so crushing.

Codeine sleep, finally. Heavy, obliterating. She doesn't groan. She doesn't dream. I lie rigid and awake, aware of alien sounds: the hum and gurgle of air conditioners, buzz of spotlights and invisible security devices — Golden Gate's protective army.

Snatches of song bounce around in my mind. A word, half a word, riding the back of a half-remembered tune. How does it go? I meant to ask earlier, but in the scramble of the day, the meals, medications, manoeuvring, I forgot. "*Wieder, Flieder...tra, la, la*." Next door she snores. The noise of over-used plumbing.

"What are you afraid of, *mein kind*?" Mother Holle spread her snow all over the world, snow like feathers in every crack and crevice, smoothing out the jagged edges, the jutting stone, tucking in the sleeping earth. I want to go back to her, to my room, kneel beside the bed and sing into the air above her head, a song that guards but doesn't wake, an old song that imitates the sigh of pines. "*Leise, leise...shhhh*."

Who will share my country when you're gone?
Who will speak my language?

One Morning in Prague

Wakened by one of those dreams that one cannot quite remember nor dismiss — a vast, formless shadow oppressing the mind — Franz Kafka rises from his plot in the Olsany Cemetery. He shakes the earth and leaf mould from his shoulders and decides to take a break from the acres of burial grounds that stretch before him. They unsettle the spirit, all these stately groves, rows of crosses, cultivated lawns and plaques dedicated to revolutionary heroes. The medieval centre of town is what he wants. A place of narrow alleys and brooding stone.

It's been a long time since he's ventured forth like this and, despite his trepidation, he boards a rattling, spark-spitting tram that hurtles toward Republican Square. He peers through dirty tram windows at landmarks new and old. The silver needle of a TV tower jabs the sky. Blunt-faced buildings pass by and then broad streets, grand, imperial facades, Gothic towers, church spires.

"*Namiesti Republiky*," drones the voice over the tramcar's loudspeaker and passengers spill out into the square. Their hurrying steps echo like distant gunfire on the cobblestones. Kafka is dismayed to see that the square has become cluttered with street vendors peddling glass beads, leather bracelets, clumsy clay models of palaces and T-shirts emblazoned with his very own *memento mori* features. A vendor waves an inviting hand to passersby. "Deutschmark? Dollar?" he asks hopefully.

Kafka quickens his pace down Celetna Street, past # 5, his childhood home, toward Old Town Square. He longs to gaze upon the procession — cathedral, town hall, palace, monument — that once held him captive with its harsh splendour. He looks forward to the aroma of dark, damp stone, the cold smell of vast halls. But the square is bustling when he arrives — tourists, street musicians, hawkers, the gaudy umbrellas of café tables encroaching upon the plaza like brilliant toadstools. The ancient facades have been freshened up, painted pink, yellow, blue. And in every corner, scaffolds and plastic sheeting, paving stones upturned, signs of restless industry, a hunger to erase years of communist neglect, a frenzy of restoration. Oh, for an undisturbed crevice to scuttle into!

He hurries toward the narrow alleys behind St. Nicholas Church, letting his footsteps take him where they may through the tortured windings of what once was Josefstadt, the ghetto. Here too he is pursued, assaulted by the smell of breakfast sausage and fried oil. But this place is quieter, and another odour — a sweet-sour ferment — wafts from cellars and drainpipes. He plunges onward until he arrives at a door in a wall, entrance to the old Jewish graveyard. He'd almost forgotten it existed.

The gatekeeper is a muttering old woman whose broad hips remind him of the masses of Babushka dolls that wobble on the street vendors' tables. She is exasperated because her arthritic fingers cannot manage the Byzantine lock in the grille across the wooden door. She twists and wrenches and rattles and still the lock's innards refuse to budge. He remembers wrestling with locks such as this one in his youth. Their cavernous keyholes swallow up puny-toothed keys.

"May I have a try?" he offers. The trick is to push the key in only partway, then ease it around, feeling for the lock's elusive pins. The grille swings open and the grateful gate-keeper allows him in without demanding the 100 Koruna admission charge.

He must ascend steps to the ancient cemetery as if ascending an altar, its ground being high above street level. He emerges from the stairwell into a forest of tombs. A riot of headstones crowded together, jostling one another, leaning this way and that, swaying and sighing with the wind, pressed up against the high cemetery walls. Under the tombstones, the earth swells, buckles, heaves. Not a flat surface, not a solid line, anywhere. The stones themselves are worn into thin lozenges, pockmarked, faded. Their engraved names and deeds are all but washed away. Some are broken in two, severed pieces drifting away from ragged stumps. Some are like drunkards about to keel over. Some are already down on the ground. This multitude cavorts in cool, dark shade under the canopy of plane trees. The trunks lean too. Long and gangly, they rear up from the ground, each craning toward a small patch of sky.

Kafka's eyes relax in the half-light. He breathes in the delicate scent of mildew, stone, moss, ancestral decay. Silence rains down upon him. Despite the press of graves, he has no trouble slipping in and out among them. They only appear to jostle. Between each, deep troughs of space and swells of time give plenty of room for the spirit to wander.

"Well, well," he says to them. "Once you were a ghetto. Now you are a sea."

His reverie is broken by a shriek of iron grille. Footsteps

clatter up the path. The first parade of visitors heaves into sight, led by their tour guide, a pretty, blond woman brandishing a tomato-red umbrella.

"The Hebrew word for cemetery is *Beit Chayim*, House of Life," she intones. "Please, ladies and gentlemen, please to stay on the path."

They file behind her. Voices exclaim, fingers point, necks crane. A man inserting film into his camera blocks the traffic and creates a bottleneck on the stairs, raising a buzz of angry murmurs. Some visitors bow their heads and whisper, place pebbles on graves when they learn from the guide that this is the custom. But try as they might to be reverent, their voices rasp. A trembling, gnarled-fingered woman reaches out to touch a stone and leaves behind sweat and tears to eat away at the ancient letters.

"In this small area you have maybe 12,000 tombstones." The tour guide pitches her voice above the murmurs and scraping feet. "But that is only tip of the iceberg." She pauses, looks around at the faces turned toward her. "Under the ground, many, many, many more graves. You see, this was only burial ground allowed to Jews for three centuries. Soon it was full. So what they do? They threw more earth on, made more graves. Underneath us right now, 12 layers of graves. There are 100,000 buried here. And as you see, the area is small." Her hand sweeps toward the encircling walls. "Please to follow me now."

Japanese, American, Israeli, German, French — they are all here, babbling in their various tongues. Their muscles twitch, their stomachs rumble, their blood gurgles with discontent or desire. Kafka must put his hands over his ears to shut out the restless, crackling energy they emit by simply shuffling forward in a long human train.

172

"The cemetery began in the 15th century and was in the centre of the ghetto. Around here are six very old and famous synagogues. They are open for you to see and there is *much* to see."

Kafka creeps behind gravestones, working his way toward a far corner of the cemetery where it might be possible to sit in peace.

"On the walls of the Pinkas Synagogue you can see names of 77,000 Czech Jews killed in Holocaust. A memorial."

Kafka rounds a corner, edges along the wall and finds his secluded nook. The tour guide's yapping blends mercifully with the chirps of jackdaws in the trees.

But, alas, here too he is not alone.

Three people — a man, woman and child — are sneaking along the wall in his direction, casting anxious glances over their shoulders at the troupe of tourists and the path that leads to the entrance gate. Kafka slips behind a stone where he can observe undetected.

The girl is about 12, the man and woman in their 30s. They are dressed in dark, out-of-fashion clothes, shabby, but probably once decent enough. The strap on the girl's left patent-leather shoe is broken and she has adopted a kind of stiff-legged gait to keep the back of the shoe from sliding down. The man is weighed down by two suitcases, one with a rope handle. He leads the way, but now stops, looks wildly around, shoots off at a tangent with the other two in tow. All three scramble and trip, get their feet stuck between the jutting stones. The man finally motions the woman and girl to follow him toward the large family vaults ranged against the wall in another far corner. They don't have far to go and they move quickly, but suddenly the old gatekeeper emerges from around the corner, chin tilted upward like a dog sniffing the air. The three rush forward. The suitcases thud against the man's knees, and it is this sound, probably, that alerts the gatekeeper to the unusual trio flitting between the trees.

"*Ahoj!*" she calls. "Stop!"

The three continue their useless flight, toppling several of the more precariously tilted stones as they scramble.

The gatekeeper bolts with startling speed on her short fat legs and cuts them off just before they reach the stone vaults.

"*Kam jdete?* Where are you going?" she demands.

"*Bitte...*," says the man, lifting his arms in a gesture that is half apology, half plea. The woman and girl stand as if welded together, the woman's arms wrapped protectively around the girl's shoulders.

It is apparent to Kafka that the trio understands not a word of the gatekeeper's Czech, just as she is utterly bewildered by their German. He steps from the shadows and bows to the group.

"Allow me to translate," he says to each party in its respective language.

"Where are their tickets?" the gatekeeper wants to know.

"*Bitte...*please," says the man. "We will not be in the way. We will be quite still." He has small twitching features, like a rabbit, and he cracks the knuckles of one hand in the clenched fist of the other as he speaks. The woman darts him a quick glance, but he keeps on.

"I believe they are in considerable distress," Kafka ventures to the gatekeeper.

"I believe they don't have tickets."

The man fishes into the inside pocket of his jacket and pulls out a wallet with some dog-eared certificates. Identity cards. Besides being in German, they are absurdly out of date.

The photos show the unsuspecting, well-fed faces of Thomas and Gretl Birnbaum and their daughter Louisa. The girl has a coquettish finger on her chin, a pose copied, no doubt, from a favourite film star.

"What am I to do with these?" The gatekeeper pushes away Thomas Birnbaum's outstretched hand without a glance at the obsolete papers. "If they want to give me the entrance fee...the full high-season rate, mind you...."

Gretl Birnbaum brings out a tightly folded wad of bills, but once unfolded, they elicit a string of curses from the gatekeeper. She has never seen bills like these before and knows immediately that they are worthless.

Thomas now falls to his knees and opens the suitcases. They are stuffed with a hodgepodge of items, clearly the work of someone who has packed in haste. Assorted pieces of clothing, galoshes, suspenders, undergarments, a fox-fur collar with red glass eyes, books, a china doll, lace doilies, a silver spice box for the end-of-Sabbath ceremony, and several large salami sausages. Gretl shakes her head. A strangled laugh bursts from her lips. Kafka suspects she was not the one who did the packing. Thomas offers the gatekeeper sausages, the fox fur and finally, with trembling hands, the spice box. She stares, indignant and inflexible, arms crossed over her chest.

From Thomas' jumbled phrases, dark hints and frantic gestures, Kafka fathoms the quest.

"They want...for a while, a short while, as long as you are willing...to stay here." Kafka points to the carved stone guarding the entrance of one of the rare aboveground tombs, no doubt quite roomy compared with the others, belonging to one of the ghetto's more illustrious families. The gatekeeper stares at him, incredulous.

Thomas leaps to his feet and speaks rapidly, hands waving. He has a high, tense voice that communicates anxiety with irritating effectiveness.

"I assure you we have money. You know the famous shoe store on the promenade in Marienbad? Mine. I own it...with my brothers, that is. Our funds are tied up at the moment but...."

"Hush! They'll hear him." The gatekeeper gestures anxiously toward the clump of visitors on the other side of the cemetery. "He'll disturb the tour."

Now Gretl Birnbaum speaks up, pushing her daughter forward, although her hands remain clamped on the girl's shoulders.

"At least take her. She will not disturb. She is so good, such a good girl." A pitiful fire blazes in the woman's large, handsome eyes. Louisa looks up, stricken, and Kafka is not sure what she fears more — the gatekeeper's acceptance or refusal.

As Kafka translates, the old woman fidgets with the fringes of her shawl, chews her cracked lips.

"Do you know how hard it is for someone like me? Keeping a job in these times? And pensions are worth nothing since the devaluation. Besides," she says in a weary tone, "what about all the others? Why bring in these three and not any of the others?"

"What others?" he whispers to the gatekeeper, feeling again the shadow that has been floating at the back of his mind all day.

"Ha! Don't tell me you don't know what I'm talking about," she says with renewed irritation. "Armies of them pressed up against the walls, mouths gaping in every crack. Long lineups in ditches and gutters across the country and every one of them has a story, why he or she or their child should be allowed in. And they've been told ages ago it's useless, there's no room, they'd overrun this place in a flash and spoil it for the visitors. And don't they all say what your friends here say?" The gatekeeper points a red forefinger at the Birnbaums. "That they just want a temporary refuge when you know full well that if you let them, they'll dig in as deep as they can and it would be hell to root them out again."

Kafka drops his head. He cannot bear to look at Gretl Birnbaum, who seems determined to fix upon him, of all people, her gaze of savage hope. He is suddenly filled with shame about his comfortable resting place at the Olsany Cemetery, not as picturesque as this one, perhaps, but perfectly adequate, and a place he can return to whenever he wishes. What petulant, childish dissatisfaction drove him to wander? Or was it this very shame about facts, which, as the gatekeeper so rightly pointed out, he'd been aware of all along? With a murmur of apology to the Birnbaums, he slinks away toward the exit just as the tour guide comes to the climax of her talk.

"Ladies and gentlemen, please. A few more words before we finish. This cemetery was closed to burials in 1787 and a new cemetery was built in the Olsany area, outside the Old Town. But these graves here, and the synagogues around them, are all that is left of Jewish ghetto of Prague. And they are oldest surviving Jewish relics in Europe. They survive because Hitler decided to make a museum here — the Exotic Museum of an Extinct Race, he called it. Some broken vaults here as you can see. Broken in the war. Maybe where the Jews hid their precious belongings before they went to concentration camps. But please to stay on the path. Don't look for treasure now. All is in State Museum with interesting explanations and displays."

Acknowledgements

Many people helped me bring this book into the world. I was honoured to study with fine writers in workshops, courses and programs. My thanks to Frances Itani, Rita Donovan, Bryan Moon, Bonnie Burnard, Robert Majzels, Jane Urquhart, Fred Stenson and Ronnie Brown. I am grateful to the writers and other friends who commented on the manuscript: Mary Borsky, Nadine McInnis, Debra Martens, Elizabeth Greene, Miriam Klein-Hanson, Susan Zettel, Cheryl Jaffee, Natalie Danford and all the members of the Ottawa Writers Group. Thank you to the Sage Hill Writing Experience, the Banff Writing Studio (especially Rachel Wyatt and Edna Alford) and John Buschek. Deep thanks to my friends and family who have encouraged me in so many ways. I am indebted to Joy Gugeler at Raincoast Books for her hard work, dedication and patience. Finally, deepest thanks to my life's companion, Barbara Freeman, who stands beside me always.

"Song of Ascent" was first published in *PRISM international* and later in the *Journey Prize Anthology*. "Breaking the Sabbath," "A Man Who Has Brothers" and "In This Corner" first appeared in *Coming Attractions 98* (the first story under the title "Premonitions," the second under the title "Calling"). "One Morning in Prague" and "Maladies of the Inner Ear" first appeared in *Parchment: contemporary Canadian Jewish writing,* and the latter story also was published in the *Journey Prize Anthology*. "Mother Tongue" and "Air and Earth" (originally "Wanderers") were first published in *Quintet*.